B|R|E|A|T|H|E

Anne-Sophie Brasme

Translated by
Rory Mulholland

 ST. MARTIN'S GRIFFIN 🙠 NEW YORK

BREATHE. Copyright © 2001 by Libraire Arthème Fayard. Translation copyright © Rory Mulholland 2003. All rights reserved. Printed in the United States of America. No part of this book may be reproduced in any manner whatsoever without written permission except in the case of brief quotations embodied in critical articles or reviews. For information, address St. Martin's Press, 175 Fifth Avenue, New York, N.Y. 10010.

www.stmartins.com

ISBN 0-312-33153-3
EAN 978-0312-33153-5

First published in Great Britain by Weidenfeld and Nicolson, a division of the Orion Publishing Group, Ltd.

First published in France by Librairie Arthème Fayard as *Respire*

10 9 8 7 6 5 4 3 2

There exists inside each of us a hidden, unknown being who speaks a foreign language and with whom, sooner or later, we have to strike up a conversation.

FRANCOIS TAILLANDIER

A cold and colourless shadow slides in from the night. It moves along the central corridor before creeping under the metal doors and into this little space enclosed by the cell walls. The same opacity comes to visit us each night, loyal, inalterable. Behind the electric wires that line the yard, we spend our hours watching the endless void that envelopes the world, but we never see any signs to tell us how far advanced the night is.

The heavy, echoing tread of departing warders marks the start of our night. After midnight no sound will trouble the silence. Solitude and alienation take hold of us. No one sleeps.

It is impossible in this place. This was one of the first things I learned when I arrived. We turn tirelessly on our mattresses, we snore, we cough or we try talking out loud, but nothing we do can break the isolation of our insomniac nights.

Some of the women cry. In the first weeks their tears are cries of revolt and of hatred. They express feelings of injustice and of sorrow. As the months and years go by the tears learn to be quiet. But they are still there, anchored in silence, and time will never wipe them away.

Some of the women seem never to have known emotion. But at night they pray. They appear insentient when they're silent, but in the dark they look up at the sky and speak to it in their secret language.

Others dream while they lie awake. Their families, their hopes, the tender indolence of their former lives, these things come to haunt them, as though to ease the agony of their wait. Sometimes they pretend they've forgotten that they're going to be shut away here for so many more years.

But I know that there's not one among us who will have the strength to fall asleep. Even I have tried and, despite all the will in the world, I cannot.

Silence is our therapy. It teaches us to look at the past, to face up to what we've done, to fight the mistakes we've made. It teaches us to reflect, it makes us question, it guides us. It can soothe our anguish or heighten it, it brings us out of incertitude or plunges us into folly. It tames us, kills the weight of the hours, fights against the selves we would rather forget.

Until the warders' steps, creaking through the corridor, tell us that a new day has begun. In reality it is the same day.

This is how nights are here, behind the bars of our detention.

Forgetting

I'd forgotten. The joy, the shamelessness, the indolence, the smells, the silences and the dizziness, the images, the colours and the sounds, their faces, the tone of their voices, their absence and their smiles, the laughter and the tears, the happiness and the impertinence, the disdain and the need for love, the taste of the first years of my life. But the past suddenly resurfaces in the depth of this darkness-soaked cell, in the chill of solitude. It confesses, at length, painfully. To counter, perhaps, the emptiness of the present. Like botched photos with blurred movements, images shatter in my memory. The truth is that I had forgotten nothing, but until now had not deigned to remember. My life might have been normal. If I'd chosen, I might've been able to live like any of you. But perhaps it wasn't really my fault: at a certain moment someone got the better of me and I was no longer master of my actions. Perhaps. I don't know.

My existence appeared flat and insignificant. I

lived in a world that did not see me, that I didn't understand. I existed because I had been made to exist. That's how it was. I should be glad to be alive, simply to be there. I was, after all, a child like any other. I lived without wondering why, I took what was given me, I asked for nothing. Yet what happened to me was inevitable. It's a well-known fact that the craziest people are those who at first sight look entirely normal. Obsession is smart: it targets those anonymous faces who look as though they haven't the slightest worry. That's what happened to me. Nothing today links me to the carefree, spirited child I was. Today, I have two identities and recognise neither.

One day someone asked me, was I sorry? I didn't reply. Maybe I was ashamed, not of what I'd done, but of what I'd felt. Surely I should have felt inhuman. I was inhuman, there's no denying it. But less for committing a crime than for not feeling regret.

My name is Charlene Boher and I'm nineteen years old. I've been stuck here nearly two years now, watching the same day go by. I was barely out of childhood when I committed the irreparable. On the night of 7 September, two years ago, I killed. I admit it. Besides, I've told the police everything. I was, as some would have it, 'totally lacking in maturity for a girl of sixteen'. But I didn't act on some wild impulse. I knew exactly what I was doing, I'd planned every detail, I was aware of the consequences. People might well despise me, they may look at me with hatred in their eyes, but I regret nothing, do you hear, not a single aspect of the events that destroyed my life. Sinking into madness is not necessarily fate, it can be a choice.

No doubt I chose not to have to look at the mistakes of the past. I fled out of cowardice, propelled by my refusal to answer the whys and the wherefores of my life, by hatred of myself. I was afraid. I feared pain, I feared truth, I feared remorse. I was afraid of having been blind and suddenly having to open my eyes. In short, I feared regret.

So I decided to write.

To transcribe my life, my almost banal past. My story began in the most deceptive innocence. I make myself piece together my memories because I realise they reveal signs of an obsession that would become incurable. I make myself remember because I need to talk.

Modesty, violence, anger make me want to talk. Pain, too. You write like you kill. It comes from the belly and all of a sudden it's in your throat. It's a cry of despair.

The first thing I remember is the scent of a blouse. I think it must have been made of silk, or at least some very fluid material, that fell down over a generous breast. It was a flowery fragrance, magnolia perhaps, sensual, with a hint of spice, like the smell of the powder women put on their faces.

The aroma came from a neck. A neck with a pearl necklace that my fingers twiddled. The neck was a little wrinkled. It belonged to a strong woman, a woman with damp skin. The woman spoke. I fell asleep in her silky arms, breathing in her scent. Maman. A thousand memories gallop in my head.

I sense the summer. I recall escapades in the cool, damp grass, four-year-old legs carrying me as fast as they can across a vast garden. I remember the smell of hay and sneezing in the dust, the rugged caress of trees, the scratches on their bark. The tender touch of the mud and the sludge mixed with the cold, pleasing water as I crossed the little stream in front of my grandparents' house, trousers pulled up over grazed knees. The syrupy taste of the first fruits of the year that we stole from a corner of the old orchard, dribbling over our tongues and sugar-sticky hands. The summer has the taste of brown earth, damp grass, sand, of burning salt.

Far from the summer there was Paris. An apartment under the roof, high walls, gigantic doors. A tangle of corridors that led to immense bedrooms where a subtle calm reigned. All was white – the tiles, the walls, the space.

I remember the silences, different according to the time of day or night, long solitudes around me in a world too vast for a child: there was the silence of the morning, the first sounds of the cars on the boulevard, the fatigue, the diffuse half-light before the shutters were opened, the tick-tock of the clock in the kitchen, the crumpling of the pages of my father's newspaper, the strange dizziness that took hold of me, like a fear, the moment he had to leave and I was left alone with the nanny. Then there was the solitude of the afternoon, the distant, muffled racket of the city streets, the hours when the apartment was empty. And there was the silence of the night, when, alone in my room, I was the last to sleep and I listened to the darkness murmuring in my ear.

I would spend hours shut in my room, watching the sun play with the shadow behind the curtains. I liked the emptiness, with me in the middle of it. It plunged me into a state of contemplation, of abandon, that made me happy and anxious at the same time. A confusion of perceptions comes to me from the apartment. My childhood tears, the taste of salt as they rolled down over my cheeks to die on my lips. Papa's voice in the half-light of my room as he told the same story every night to put me to sleep, the story I knew word for word, the contact of his nascent beard on my forehead as he bid me goodnight and I pretended to doze. The pillow fights with my brother, the silly nonsense, the frolicking on the bed, the thousand quarrels that always ended in bursts of laughter.

What sort of a child was I?

A tormented one, my mother always said. A turbulent, cheeky kid, not normal. Perhaps. My mother talked too much. Often to say how unhappy she was. I remember a difficult little girl full of enthusiasm and passion. An unsociable, intrepid little girl, a girl who often embarrassed her parents, a child whose parents could not control her. Everywhere I went people remembered the little pest with the impossible temperament, the girl who screamed in public or pulled other children's hair or made impertinent replies to grown-ups. I loved life. I devoured it. Which wasn't easy for my mother.

My fits of anger would be followed by a need for solitude, by hours of calm. I had lots of love to give. But I was much too alone.

I didn't understand the world. I found it a strange place; I didn't exist, it seemed that everything I could see or touch, hear or feel, was without substance. I was living in a world of silence and questions, of abstraction, of games and cries, of laughter and tears, of joy and light, but I had control over nothing.

Every childhood has its fragrance, its dizziness, its pains. I remember my childhood as I remember fear.

The very first years of my existence were filled with the presence of an imaginary character who appeared each night in the same dream. It was a small woman who moved against an orange background, her silhouette tiny and fragile, her hair short, her clothes luminous. Far behind her was a swarm of faceless, voiceless persons. After a certain time I didn't want her to come any more, I told her to go but she insisted on staying till I fell asleep. It was, I think, the moment she finally decided to leave me that my fear emerged.

I dreamt that the floor fell away from beneath me, that I could no longer walk, that the world around me refused to move forward. People came up to me and as soon as they tried to talk to me, they began frothing at the mouth and the words they wanted to say were choked in slaver.

My fears soon multiplied. There was a monster hiding in the shadows of my room; when night fell I huddled under the bedclothes and whispered imploring words to placate it. Then came the woman in white who appeared in the mirror as soon as the light was turned off. I feared her wan, expressionless face, so every night till I was fifteen years old, I turned the mirror to face the wall.

Would I have turned out a different person had my family circumstances been different? My parents did love me. Perhaps they loved me too much, but in a way that was less emotional than material. I still wonder why they tried so desperately to create meaning out of the void that was my life. I'd asked for nothing. I would have preferred if they'd hated me, as I probably deserved. My fall would then have been less painful, both for me and for them.

Maman was a practical woman, very down-to-earth. She wanted everything to be perfect. To me she was like a block of ice. Of course, when you're five years old, you're not hugely aware of the world around you. A few hugs and a toy from time to time is enough to make you happy. But later came much deeper needs to which my mother was not able to respond. I loved her, but certainly not as I should have done. As I grew, I became for her the other side of the wall. On the day of my conviction she collapsed in the courtroom and started shouting that *it was her that I'd killed*. They had to take her out and give her some tablets. I think that was the last time I saw her. I'd lost the scent of her perfume long before then.

As for my father, it was his absences that frustrated me. His work, his passion, his *obligations*, as he put it. All of which means that today I have only furtive memories of him, distant images, the absent father, the father who forgets, the father who has *other priorities*. And yet I don't remember suffering on account of his insufficient presence. Perhaps I didn't really care. You get used to anything. The only image that comes to mind when I think of him is that seemingly endless mahogany door, the door to his office, the door of his exile, that forbidden entrance that kept us apart. Papa is now the only one, along with my brother, who comes to see me in prison; through the glass in the visiting room I see his face puffy with age, and each time I feel we're growing less strange to each other.

Later there was school. I must have been five or six. I see corridors with blue walls decorated with ugly children's drawings and large windows looking out onto a yard. I hear cries, laughter, voices in the silence of the blue corridors.

I have a strange and bitter memory of the place. I was a good pupil, but I was often turbulent, impetuous, cheeky. In short, I was the type of kid teachers hated, the one they kept apart from the others, the one they put at the back of the class.

One day a little girl who looked like a blue bonbon came along to brighten up my life. She was called Vanessa. She was a bit tubby – I was scrawny – and she had very long hair that was always impeccably plaited and a doll's face dotted with freckles and lit up by immense forget-me-not eyes. In contrast I was a real tomboy, always scruffy, my hair a mess.

It is, I think, the first intact image that remains of my past. Our eyes met in the toilets of the Jeunes Sourires nursery school. Her smile fascinated me. I was thunderstruck. I've never really known what made the blue bonbon want to be friends with the little monster, but from that day on we were always together. Those few years we spent together brought us so close that soon we could no longer even imagine living separate lives.

I called her every Saturday morning at seven, which drove her mad. My heart thumping and my hand trembling, I'd dial the number and wait to hear her little voice. We talked about our dreams, our imaginary lives, we sang nursery rhymes to each other, we laughed. Nothing could shut us up. We always had something to share, to tell each other, and when we had nothing more to say we'd make things up. What mattered was that we understood each other.

She would invite me over to her house. I remember her bedroom, where the wallpaper was the same colour as her eyes. I can still see the soft light in the room, the little window that looked out onto the street, the periwinkle-blue eiderdown covering the bed, the wardrobe at the end of the room, the child's drawings on the walls, the unruly piles of toys. This was our universe.

It was extraordinary to see the world through her eyes. My dreams were her dreams. It took only a word, a look, sometimes no more than a moment's silence, for us to understand each other. Nothing could break the bonds of our friendship. Our worlds were one and the same. We lived on a distant planet, far from all the others, but what counted was that we were no longer alone.

Vanessa was my best friend for almost six years. She was my security, my fortune, my light. She protected me. She was the sunshine of my childhood. I remember her soothing presence, the hours spent at her side, the adventures, the stories, the murmurs in the half-light of the afternoon. I remember her smell, which even today I still cannot define, but which I call 'le parfum bleu' on account of her big, enigmatic eyes. Vanessa was a blue perfume. Vanessa was a blue flower. Vanessa was a blue angel. All this has no real connection to the story that follows. Or perhaps it does. Vanessa eventually went away, and when she did I desperately needed to fill the gap she left. Vanessa was much more than a passing phenomenon in my childhood. She's the only person who has always stayed close to me. I don't know what's become of her, but I know she's still there for me. When you're barely five years old you don't have the words to say such things, but there was no doubting even then that we'd made each other a secret promise. One day during the trial when I turned to face the gallery I was able to look into her immense opal eyes which, almost fifteen years later, looked into my heart just as they did when we were kids.

That part of my life now seems inconsequential, lacking in substance. My childhood was a strange one. In the mad world that surrounded me I could see only my own little universe.

It was perhaps this need for isolation, this failure to understand other people, which made me begin writing. One day – I was maybe eight – I asked my mother to buy me a notebook. I began to fill its pages with crude and uncertain handwriting. Putting my stories down on paper, creating characters, recording my dreams, was merely one game among the many I played. I loved inventing heroes for my tales, giving them a face and a history – princesses with broken hearts, brave and love-struck knights, evil witches bent on cruel deeds. I lived with these creations, their almost palpable presence helped me forget my solitude.

The child that I was haunts my memory. Writing, now much more than a simple pleasure, much more than a need, has become my truth, my sole defence against reality.

That childhood is here, buried deep within the walls of this cell. And alongside the pleasant memories are many furtive, disturbing, unwanted images.

A scene comes to mind. The large apartment, evening, winter. Night-time. I hear cries. Tears, blows, sudden movements. My brother Bastien's arms protect me. But he trembles as much as I do.

I must have been about seven when my parents' first fights marked the start of the slow destruction of our family. There were sleepless nights as I lay weeping in my room listening to them scream. I see my mother stretched out on the sofa, trying to hold back her sobs. I see my father sitting at his desk, impassive and silent after the storm.

I never really knew what they were fighting about. They never told me anything, I was still too young to understand grown-up things. Later it became a family taboo to mention such incidents. One day I asked Maman if she was still in love with the man my father was so angry about. There was a long silence, then a look of desolation and a nod of the head. For an instant I hated her with all the hatred that there is in the heart of a child.

After that I don't know. There was so much uncertainty in our family life. A period when there was little that held us together. My parents were opposed to divorce, so for years we lived together as strangers. I observed the family tableau: the mother driven mad, the brother forever silent, the eternal absence of the father. And where was I? I was nowhere. I was external to them and to their problems. My life was lived against a backdrop of pain. Thus it was that our family slowly, silently destroyed itself.

I began to grow up.

To my parents I pretended I was horrified by the idea. I sulked when my mother suggested I buy a bra or when she tried to explain what having my first period would be like. For years I spurned affection, especially when it came from Maman. I became a wall of ice. I couldn't bear anyone to touch me, even look at me. I didn't need anyone's love.

The truth was that I longed for my body to be

transformed. I burned with jealousy when Vanessa began to change. While her body showed the first signs of womanhood, my own clung stubbornly to childhood. I stood every day in front of the bathroom mirror and scoured my flesh for anything that might suggest I was finally about to enter puberty. Nothing. My stomach remained bloated like that of a child – even though in my head I was convinced that I was no longer one – and my chest remained resolutely flat.

I felt stifled. Oppressed by my body, by my parents, by the eyes of others, I felt like spitting on the world.

Misunderstood, unloved, I screamed silently. On a whim I decided to stop writing. Within an hour my vengeance had destroyed my notebooks and my stories. I blamed my parents, I was convinced that they only loved me for what I wrote. Often my mother would proudly recount my stories to her friends, boasting that she had a prodigy on her hands. My gesture of contempt was designed to show them that I was more than just a precocious child destined to be a writer. I was begging them to see me as their daughter, nothing more.

My parents were worried. One day soon after the book-destroying episode I found myself in the grim office of a psychologist. I remember the half-darkness of the room, I remember sitting opposite this inaccessible man who peered down on me as I looked defiantly up at him. We had two or three sessions, he asked me some stupid questions to which I gave frosty answers, he concluded that it was a passing phase, there was no need to be worried. If he'd known what was to become of me ten years later he might not have been so reassuring.

It was the worst thing in the world when Vanessa left. But her departure, when we were about eleven, was a well-earned punishment for years of making others suffer and thinking only of myself.

I remember the day we said goodbye. It was August, the sun was burning, the wind blowing. She had to keep pushing her long, thick brown hair off her face. Her eyes had never seemed so big nor so blue. It hurt me to see her cry. It felt like a knife in my chest. In her hand she held the pendant I'd given her for her last birthday. It was the figure of a little blue dancer. The day before, we had mixed our blood and promised to remain friends forever.

I threw my arms around her and held her tightly. Her blue perfume submerged me and I cried as though I'd suddenly understood the true meaning of tears. I cried because I knew we wouldn't be able to keep our promises.

After a long embrace Vanessa stood back a little and smiled at me. Then she turned and got into the car, which slowly disappeared in the dust. I cried, I cried for weeks, I cried cruel tears that burned my face. Then I faced up to the distress of my solitude.

Vanessa's departure marked the end of my childhood. I was eleven years old. I decided I had to move on, I had to grow, I had to blossom. No more tantrums, no more childish conceit. In September I was due to start at Chopin College, a posh school I'd been accepted for after sitting a tough entrance exam. My parents had been dead set on me going there, and I was too. I wanted to be the best on all fronts. I saw study as a way of getting over the death of the friendship that had eased me through childhood.

On 6 September I walked through the school gate and into the yard. I looked straight ahead and swore that I would be the best, at any price.

Suffocating

I remember that September morning with extraordinary clarity. The damp scent of autumn, the
colourless sky, the grey of the streets, the hum of
the boulevards, the tender fatigue of the morning.

The cold, menacing, squalid school building
seemed to rise higher as I approached. The debris of
my detested adolescence – those painful years, the
loneliness, the waiting – is somehow inextricably
linked to this insipid image of my first day in
secondary school.

I stood there, all of one metre fifty tall, fragile,
struggling under my schoolbag, and raised my eyes
towards the dull walls of the school, horribly alone
and scared stiff at the idea of having to do this
without Vanessa at my side.

I entered a large yard that swarmed with hundreds of unknown faces. I felt tiny in the dreadful
throng that formed around me. I spotted a sign for
my class: Group 2. Around twenty students stood
below it in front of one of the doors and waited for

a teacher. I joined the group, carefully avoiding catching anyone's eye.

It was a truly horrible day. The first thing they told us was that we'd been through a rigorous selection process, that we were now part of the élite and that it was out of the question that we should be anything but the best. Sink or swim, was what they were really saying.

Then came weeks and months of hard work, fatigue and despondency. Our class was, of course, one of the best in Chopin. But the workload was impossible for children who were barely twelve years old. It exhausted me. I was consistently getting A grades, but I lived in fear of a run-in with a teacher or a fall to the level of 'unsatisfactory'.

I'd get home from school in a terrible state. I have grim memories of trudging through the dead leaves on rue Chopin, in the freezing cold, an invisible weight cutting into my shoulders.

That first school year seemed endless.

I had few friends. The few students who did accept me in their group were among the best in the class. I thought they were morons. Our conversations never ranged beyond our neat little lives in our posh little school. I was simply playing a role, and I hated the character I'd chosen. I couldn't under-stand the others, I found their talk and their aspirations pathetic. I never really fitted in. So it was no surprise that I soon found myself completely on my own. Which was, I suppose, what I'd really wanted from the start.

I thought it was contempt that I felt for my classmates, but now I see that it was merely indifference. The boredom of the classes, the slowness of each day and hour was unbearable. Nothing provided relief from the stifling routine. Everything seemed sordid. I often had a lump in my throat that blocked my breath. The ache within me was a cry of impotence that no one ever heard.

And at the same time there was my puberty, late and painful.

March. It's PE class, we're at the pool. In the changing room, after an exhausting hour in the water, I discreetly look at the other girls' naked bodies. I am not like them, I am thin and bony. My face is pointed and sombre. It has no sparkle, no smile, no light. I hate my abnormal, pre-pubescent body. I feel dirty, useless. I envy their happy faces, their shimmering hair, their skin that smells of baby powder. Grace comes naturally to them. Not to me. I observe their voluptuous figures and consider mutilating my body. I look at my reflection in the mirror and see an ugly shadow. Wet locks falling down over nasty spots and an icy face. My yellowish skin and greasy hair disgust me. I hate myself so much that I feel like spitting on the mirror and then smashing it. I'm afraid. I dream of being someone else, of growing up, of being free.

I'm almost thirteen and haven't had a period. Maybe I'll never be an adult. When I cry in my bed at night I can almost hear a chorus of chanting: 'You're a monster, Charlene. A monster. Why don't you kill yourself? You'd be better off dead.'

One day I tried. Just to see how they'd react.

It's Monday and we have to go to the third floor. The narrow stairwell makes me feel trapped, stifled by the crush of students. I decided I'd had enough. Slowly, gently, I let myself go. I felt like I was disappearing, like I was being swallowed up by the crowd. I fell back and rolled down the steps. I closed my eyes and smelled the ground, felt feet crushing me, stepping on my hair. When my fall was complete I remained still, my nose in the dust, tears in my eyes, and I felt even dirtier and more ridiculous than ever. A teacher came and picked me up. I pretended I'd had a dizzy spell. She held my hand and helped me to the infirmary. There I waited for my mother to come and take me home. I shut myself in my room and waited for someone to come and feel sorry for me and for ever take me away from this unjust life.

My view of the world began to change towards the middle of the year. I sought calm, I sought regeneration. I knew I wasn't cut out for the life I was leading and I felt I could somehow reawaken the happy Charlene that was somewhere inside me. So to keep my unpleasant reality at bay I took to dreaming. But these were dreams in which my eyes remained wide open. In bed at night I'd concoct improbable stories with me as the doughty heroine. My spirit was transported to a perfect body, a woman's body. My step was so certain that I could have faced down an entire army. This Charlene was dazzling, almost haughty, disdainful. In an instant I was able to become the woman I so longed to be. Now I wanted just one thing: to grow up. I doggedly awaited the moment when my body would finally blossom, would give birth to a girl who was infinitely more charming, more subtle, more loved. Nothing would be as before. I was convinced that by growing up the hatred inside me would give way to love.

My first year at Chopin came to an end and with it my long ordeal.

The summer that followed had the scent of thyme and lavender, of yellow dust and dirt tracks, it had a dazzling sky and vines as far as the eye could see. My parents rented an apartment in a remote Provence village near the jagged rocks of Mont Ventoux. There I learned the languor of hours spent in the sun, with the sweet smell of sun cream mixed with chlorine from the swimming pool. I think I was happy. I felt my body slowly transform itself, I felt the flower in me blossom. I took to looking at myself in mirrors, I smiled, I began to live.

We took our breakfast on the apartment terrace

each morning and I would listen to the gentle silence, the first stirrings of the mistral, the hum of the locusts. Life here, far from the oppression of Paris, was thrilling and vibrant. I began writing again, songs this time. And for the first time in my life I had a circle of friends, most of them older than me. We spent our evenings sitting in a circle by the deserted pool, humming old hits while someone strummed a guitar. Suddenly I was no longer different to everyone else. I was no longer happy just to exist: I was living, I held happiness in my hands. One night, as the first rays of moonlight cut through the darkness of my room, I felt a warm and tender pain deep within me. It persisted through the night, flowing into my stomach with limpid violence. When day came I found a cloud of blood on the white sheets. Now that I'd had my first period I could begin a new life.

Two weeks later, as our car left behind it an untamed Provence, I felt free for the first time in my life. The lump in my throat was gone. I'd grown up. My body had at last decided to germinate. Now all I needed was for others to respect me. So I made an oath to myself, I swore that when I got back to school I would be liked.

It was a beautiful, red-tinged, picturesque autumn. I arrived at the gates of Chopin emboldened by the secret promise I'd made to myself. This year I'd be different, I'd behave like a normal teenager, I'd blend in.

This was the challenge I'd set myself, my revenge on the terrible year I'd just endured. I was determined to sweep away the past and finally become someone. It was the end of the invisible Charlene. Soon others would admire and envy me. Already I imagined their surprise as I walked into the schoolyard: 'It's amazing how she's changed . . .'

I'd been waiting to get back to school the way someone else might look forward to getting out of jail. The day before I'd pictured the scene right down to the most trivial detail, how I'd talk, how I'd be more direct in my language, how I'd walk, my head held high, ready to take on the world. I was no longer weak, I was one of the group now. The others would be hideously jealous of me, of my every gesture, of my every word. I imagined them dumbfounded as I marched into the yard, pretending I didn't hear their mutterings. I'd programmed every moment of my new life, a life in which the pains of the past and the weight of my reputation were forever banished.

The long-awaited morning arrived.

I walked slowly towards a group of students from my class who stood waiting at one of the doors. Each step I took towards them thumped in my chest to the same rhythm as the beat of my heart. My confidence grew as I drew closer. I stopped in front of the little circle they formed and almost bellowed 'Bonjour.'

Nobody noticed me. I scanned the group, noting the bronzed skin and the new outfits. Some of them I barely recognised, they'd grown so much, they'd become adolescents in the space of just one summer. How I hated them! And I hated myself for being so pathetic next to their perfect teenage bodies.

I said nothing, consoling myself with the thought that I could hardly expect them to be interested in me, given that last year I'd been so stand-offish. They'd soon see just how *different* I now was.

Then I noticed someone new in the group. Everyone was listening to her. She spoke with such assurance and energy that the others seemed to drink in her words. I moved a little closer to see what she was like. Her face wasn't that pretty. It was bony, her nose was hooked and her skin was too pale, and on top of all that she had a shock of red hair. Physically she didn't have much going for her. But she had this incredible charm. Maybe it was her magnetic gaze that gave her a sort of mystique. Or maybe it was that limpid voice, the sort you could listen to for hours. She was talking about a trip to the United States, about her childhood in San Francisco, about a lot of different things. Everyone was engrossed. I didn't believe a word. I hated this girl who'd managed to hypnotise the entire class within minutes of arriving at our school.

I later learned she was called Sarah. Apparently she had spent her childhood in California before returning to Paris, the city of her birth. From that very first day I was convinced she would thwart all my ambitions. I was right. But back then I had no idea just how much more she'd do.

So. Sarah had come into my life. And she's never really left it.

I didn't keep my promise to myself. I didn't have the time. Sarah turned up and swept away everything in her path: my dreams, my aspirations, all the goals I had set myself. She monopolised attention wherever she went. She acted like she owned everything. She did exactly as she pleased. I watched and said nothing. I once again became a shadow of myself. A wall separated me from the others. I'd have preferred them to spit in my face than to abandon me like this. Indifference is worse than contempt. The feeling that you no longer exist.

They disgusted me. So did Sarah. I hated seeing them gathered around her, hearing them talk about her as if she were some sort of goddess, almost begging for a moment of her attention, acting like zombies under her control. Their naivety horrified me. 'She's nothing without your admiration,' I told myself. 'And you've all fallen for it. You're so thick.'

I slowly let myself go. I didn't bother much

about schoolwork and my marks went into a nosedive. My parents started to worry, particularly when I took to alternating between bulimia and anorexia. Sometimes I'd stick two fingers down my throat and make myself vomit until I bled, hoping that my whole body would follow the half-digested food down the toilet.

I thought a lot about death. I was fascinated by the idea of a transparent body deprived of breath and of movement, even if I didn't understand what exactly this meant. I sometimes contemplated the sinuous tangle of veins around my wrists and was tempted to take a knife and slice through them. Death was perhaps the easiest way out. But it was also the most cowardly way to avoid having to confront the indifference, the weight, the anguish of life. An awful feeling of failure haunted me. What was the point of going on if it meant merely existing?

The only thing that stopped me was the pain it would cause my parents. Sometimes I'd have a glimmer of hope and would tell myself that it was ridiculous to get so upset about something that was so insignificant and probably also temporary.

Then one day I finally cracked.

It was November, and our sports teacher would take us out for runs. We had to jog for kilometres through the streets and along the banks of the Seine, freezing in our track suits, our feet numb and our cheeks whipped by an icy wind. I always lagged behind. My asthma blocked my breath. I felt it catch in my throat and struggle out in little blasts of white steam. My lungs were constricted by each breath I took. I felt my body weaken and my legs falter. It was as though I could no longer feel my own skin. These runs were torture for me. I was terrified I would collapse, drained by the effort and suffocated by lack of air. I often held my tube of Ventoline in my hand as I ran, to reassure myself that if necessary it could give me a second wind and save me from this oppression.

That morning it was particularly cold. The Seine was covered in a thick veil of mist, as though the low temperatures were making the immobile water evaporate. I looked at the reddish horizon and the transparent sky, I saw the bare trees lining the footpaths, and as I ran I listened to the first sounds of the streets and inhaled the scent of gas and concrete that came up from the boulevard.

We were moving along the river and I could feel my muscles retracting until it seemed they couldn't move any more. My heartbeat slowed as my constricted lungs struggled to draw in oxygen. A whistling sound was coming out of my mouth. My brain laboured with each step, I felt my stomach wrenching and imagined my organs were bleeding. I felt the Ventoline in my pocket rub against my thigh and I repeated to myself: 'You don't need Ventoline, you don't need to breathe. Hang in there, Charlene, don't be afraid. Just let your legs keep moving.'

Each step I took brought me closer to the end. Every time I breathed in, the air burned my throat before it reached my ribcage with a violent pain. The irregular thump of my heart resounded deep inside me with astonishing clarity. I kept going. I wanted to experience the sensation of watching oneself die.

'The Ventoline, Charlene, the Ventoline. It's right there, in your pocket. We need it,' my lungs shouted at my brain.

'No,' I told them. 'Wait. We're nearly there. Soon you won't need any air at all, trust me.'

And then everything went white. I felt the taste of blood rise up from my chest to caress my mouth, I felt its wet and cruel kiss on my tongue. I knew I'd succeeded, that there was no going back now. The sky had become so bright that I had to close my eyes, but the white light still blinded me. Now I had only to let myself go, slowly, gently, silently. Distant voices cried: 'Charlene? Are you all right? She's not breathing. Watch out, she's going to fall!' Then there was silence.

Through the silence came a murmur. *Breathe, Charlene. Breathe.*

Then I fell. I felt my body drop slowly to the ground and felt deep pleasure along with a sense of accomplishment. I let pain take over. I felt the breath of death struggle with the breath of life, I felt it conquering each part of my being. I could see death, it was alive within me. My last thought was that I had won.

When I opened my eyes, my eyelids heavy and my mouth furry, an oxygen mask on my face, I saw that I'd been defeated yet again. My body was not dead. I was a coward. The thought of having to go out and face the world again disgusted me.

My mother was crying. My cold, inert hand lay in her warm palm. My father stood by my bed, impassive as ever. He looked exhausted, with huge bags under his red eyes. I saw my brother sitting on a black leather armchair at the back of the room. He held his head in his hands, his fingers plunged into the dishevelled black hair that fell down over his face. We cried silently.

They stayed with me all that day, and the days that came after. My mother held my hand for hours on end and this helped me feel stronger. I waited for night-time to cry. I cried because I was going to live again and the thought made me dizzy. But I had at least realised that I loved my family, and that I had almost done something irreparable. The days went by, I felt death slowly abandon me and life return. My throat burned, but the burning was not that of suffocation: it was simply the taste of my tears.

I spent my days looking at the white of the walls. It was a perfect white: sharp, limpid, soothing, vital. I was breathing again, and I suddenly realised how intensely pleasurable it was to feel the air enter me and fill my lungs before invading my entire body. The white of the walls and the oxygen I sucked in gave me a pure sensation of lightness, of infinity, of well-being. I felt like I was floating, like I was flying above myself. I wasn't thinking of tomorrow.

One day someone appeared in the half-open door. In the brilliant light of the afternoon I at first thought it was an angel. The silhouette became a person as it moved towards the bed. It was Sarah.

She placed a huge bouquet of flowers on my bedside table and explained that it was from the entire class as well as the teachers. She sat down by the bed. She spoke for a long time and I listened avidly. Her voice was clear and poised. I felt as though each of her words tamed me a little. For a moment I felt understood, I felt safe.

She looked at me and I felt like a strange light was penetrating me. She said: 'You've intrigued me ever since I arrived at Chopin. You're so solitary, so silent, so closed. I know you're unhappy, that's pretty obvious. You've got no one. And I know how you ended up here. It was no accident, was it? You knew that with your asthma they couldn't make you run if you didn't want to, and that you could stop whenever you needed to. But you didn't, did you, and you knew how it would all end. I see all that. I understand.'

I was dumbfounded, I didn't know what to say.

She had moved me. I lowered my gaze so as not to have to see the cruel truth in Sarah's eyes.

She placed her hands in mine and said nothing for a moment, while I tried to hold back my tears. Then she went on.

'You were lucky. I want you to know that you can count on me from now on. I'd like to help you. I'd like you to be my friend.'

Behind her words I was sure I could hear: 'You'll never be alone again, Charlene.'

Breathing

Nobody but Sarah had a clue about what had really happened. Not even my parents suspected that it was no accident, that it was a desire to know death, a longing to be stifled.

When the sliding doors of the hospital drew aside to release me back into the world, I had but one thing on my mind: a need to rediscover life, to be reborn, to breathe. I was ready to exist for real this time. I was ready to live. And now I had Sarah. I didn't have to face life on my own.

I was the centre of attraction as soon as I walked into the schoolyard. Sympathetic smiles and kind words came at me from all sides. The four days in hospital had created a new Charlene. So happiness did really exist. It was here, with me, and I was with Sarah. I no longer needed death as a safeguard. Now death was merely an insurance policy, an emergency exit, in case things went badly wrong.

Sarah had become my guarantee, my shelter, my light. I knew she was there for me, and I was certain that if my life went off the rails again she'd come to my help. She'd promised to be my friend.

A few days was all it took for her to become my daily dose of happiness, my victory over life. I couldn't wait to see her at the school gates, I trembled when I finally saw her walking down the street towards me each morning before joyfully throwing myself into her arms. I felt an almost frantic sort of bliss, nothing else mattered once she, my benefactor, was there to silence my old fears.

Sarah invited me to her house one day during the February holidays. My mother dropped me off at the door of an apartment block in the 12th *arrondissement*. This was where Sarah lived, in a decidedly untidy little apartment. The main room seemed exceptionally bright in the winter sunshine. A large picture window looked out over the city. The leafless branches of the trees on the boulevard brushed the windows and the sun caressed the last traces of snow. I remember walls as white as those in the hospital, the shining, turkey-red wood of the old kitchen, the bare living room that had only a sofa and a television sitting on the floor, the dusty little pieces of vaguely Chinese furniture near the window, the midnight-blue tiles in the bathroom, the collection of miniature perfume bottles and the make-up products scattered on the ledge of the porcelain sink. A heavy aroma of incense hung in the room, enough to turn your head if you breathed in too much of it.

There was a strange atmosphere in Sarah's apartment. Hours passed as though time did not exist. A deep feeling of calm, an impalpable vertigo filled me each time I set foot in her home.

We spent the afternoon together and I think I've never laughed as much in my life. We went to the park next to her building. The sky was blue and the air mild. She lay down in the grass and I joined her. The sun warmed our faces even though it was the middle of winter. I felt great. We breathed the air deep into our lungs, I smelt the earth and the dew in the quivering of my nostrils. We laughed till we were out of breath. Now when I close my eyes I can again hear the sparkle of her voice, I see her face drowning in her tousled hair and her eyes lit up by the sun. I don't know if I was laughing so much that I cried or if I was crying because I was so happy. I hadn't felt like this since childhood. Or maybe I'd never felt like this ever.

In the evening we lay down on her bed, which was a mattress laid on the floor. The window shutters streaked the bedroom with fine lines of grey light. A strange silence reigned. We could hear the sounds of outside, the last cars on the boulevard. Night assailed the world. Everything seemed infinitely peaceful. Our murmurs were lost in the immense and impenetrable calm. I felt fatigue overcome me, our voices slowly faded. We had talked a lot, especially Sarah. I had listened to her voice grow less and less audible as it pierced the quiet of the night. I listened and it seemed to me that in the space of one night I knew Sarah as well as if I'd spent my life with her.

Morning came. I opened my eyes. She was still sleeping, her body almost against mine. Her long hair was by my face, I breathed in its smell. She didn't wake up for another hour, and I spent the time watching her sleep. Breakfast lasted two hours. We chatted about everything and anything and we laughed till we nearly choked on our baguettes plastered with butter and jam.

Towards midday my father came to pick me up. We were still in our pyjamas when he arrived. I quickly dressed, grabbed my things and said good-bye to Sarah and her mother. They both said I could come back whenever I wanted, their door was always open to me. I gave Sarah a big hug. She still had the smell of morning on her, the scent of fresh sheets, of tender sweat and of sugared coffee. And so I left the little apartment that had filled me with light and with a thousand indescribable sensations.

Sarah had lived with her mother Martine, and sometimes with her 'stepfathers', in the four-room flat in a remote part of the 12th *arrondissement* ever since they'd come back from the States. Her father had been out of the picture for years and now she never even mentioned him. Her parents had divorced when she was very young and she'd been through the horrible business of the fights and the lawyers and the court cases. Her mother had apparently tried to kill herself after her two divorces and had given her kids to their grandparents to look after before deciding to take them with her to California. She was a tortured soul. Often she'd get home really late at night. Sarah and I would sit in the dark and wait up for her. We'd hear the door creak and her laughter cut through the silence. Then she'd march down the hall and the giggles would continue till dawn. We'd see her in the morning when we got up, her face exhausted as she left her room followed by a man we'd usually never seen before. I was shocked at first. Sarah said she didn't care.

Sarah didn't have many possessions. I suppose if I was middle class, she must have been what you'd call lower middle class. That didn't stop me from envying her madly. On the emotional front, she was spoilt rotten. Her grandparents adored her and her mother's friends treated her like their own daughter. And then, of course, there were all her schoolfriends. As for Martine, she insisted that their bond was more one of friendship than a mother-daughter relationship. Which meant that for several years I couldn't help but see the woman as my most dangerous rival.

My life could not have been more different to Sarah's. Our families' lifestyles were miles apart. Their daily routine – if you could call it a routine – was a total disaster, while my parents' approach ensured that each minute of my day was accounted for. I'd never known anyone as disorganised as Sarah. She and Martine had a motto that was an entirely new concept for me: 'Take it easy.' They would, for example, often get up in the late morning, decide to have lunch in the middle of the afternoon and then spend the evening at a friend's place before coming home in the early hours to snatch a few hours' sleep before heading off to work or school. Sarah often dragged me into their hectic way of doing things, which my mother found intolerable. But I didn't care. I was never again going to let my parents impose on me their drab, old-fashioned way of life.

Soon my father's car was dropping me off outside Sarah's place almost every week. Her mother adored me, and I was happy to be adopted. Their quiet little apartment became a second home for me. But we actually didn't spend that much time there. When I went round there Sarah would usually whisk me off to some smoky party or dinner at friends of her mother. My mother didn't like that either, but Sarah simply laughed in her face. So did I.

Sarah taught me how to live. She'd undone the knot that for so long had restricted my breath.

Little by little I came to know her. But she was the type of person you could never really work out. She was just too different to everyone else. She'd sometimes forget that we were thirteen and would act like an indolent child. Then she'd switch to adult mode and launch into a debate that revealed astonishing maturity. She talked for hours about her ambitions, her dreams, her fears. At times she'd have me aching with laughter at her childish exuberance, then she'd become deadly serious as she confided in me. At these moments I'd have given my life to be able to find the right words to console her.

How can I describe this girl who was like no other, this girl who changed my life? Some memories come to me. I see her standing half-naked in front of the mirror, her back to me. She has interminable legs, a boy's austere and sinewy body, the cheeky face of a street urchin. Yet her loose hair and her bare shoulders reveal a femininity whose charms are irrefutable. I watch her, dazzled. She examines herself in the mirror. She is sulky, silent, almost severe. She complains of hips that are too straight and breasts that are too small. I sit on the sofa-bed and try to comfort her, telling her how attractive she is, that she's no reason to be worried. She acts like she hasn't heard me, then suddenly turns to me and bursts out laughing before covering me in kisses.

She fascinated me. I was intrigued by her nerve, her moodiness, her candour. No one understood her better than me. I knew her by heart, I could predict her reactions, I could anticipate her moods. Yet I could never quite completely get to the bottom of her unique and contradictory character. I also admitted to myself in some despair that I would never match up to what she expected from me.

Without knowing it, Sarah was giving me an identity. When I was with her I felt I at last commanded respect, that I was even loved, and this was a new, exalting, breath-taking feeling.

I felt like I'd come alive again because of the confidence she inspired in me. She kept telling me I was 'fantastic' and that I underestimated myself, she said I was 'the friend she'd always been looking for'. I wished I could believe her. She called me Charlie and laughed like a child. Her every word brought me satisfaction. I tried so hard to be the Charlene she wanted me to be.

Sarah understood me better than I had ever understood myself. She looked beyond the simple parameters of my existence. Little by little my life took shape and I became somebody. But I was often frightened. It was all too sudden, too new, too sublime to really be happening to me.

One evening in the spring as we were heading home from school I turned to her and asked: 'Why me?' I'd tried hard to understand, but I couldn't figure out what a girl like her could see in someone like me. She had everything, and I had nothing. Everywhere she went people fell under her spell. So why hadn't she got rid of me before now?

She stopped, turned her hazy eyes to me, and said: 'But you're my best friend, Charlie.'

She said it with such frankness and calm that I believed her.

I needed her insouciance. In many ways she was still a child, whereas I had been stubbornly trying to live and think like an adult. With Sarah I rediscovered the joys of childhood. The time I spent with her had the delicious taste of forbidden things. I was bewitched, nothing could remove me from the benevolent power she exerted over me. My parents began to worry. My mother thought Sarah was a bad influence. I was horrible to them. One day, after they'd been giving me grief about my attitude, I screamed: 'Anyway, Sarah's family is *my* family. From now on you lot don't exist for me.'

Sarah and I spent part of the holidays together. It was a marvellous, sun-drenched summer. Each day the sky seemed to grow more blue. We shared a world without limits, without taboos. I *existed*. Life offered itself to me in a precious jewel case that until then I'd never dared to open.

Sometimes she came to my home and we'd spend a few days in my uncle's house in the country. There we'd roll up our trousers and chat endlessly as we splashed about in the little stream that ran through the garden.

'Give me a piggy-back, Charlie, go on!' she'd shout, knowing that I couldn't say no to her. So I'd let her climb up and hear her laugh hysterically when I collapsed into the chilly water after a couple of faltering steps. Then we'd strip off and stretch out in the grass and bake in the blazing sun. Passers-by would stare at us in shock. Sarah couldn't have cared less, and I laughed along with her. Afterwards we'd head back to the house and make up endless excuses to explain the wet trousers and the filthy shoes to my aunt.

We did all this because it was what she wanted to do. She was delighted that I did everything she said, even if it meant making me look ridiculous, even if she was the only one who found it funny. I only ever felt sure of myself when I heard her laugh. Victory for me was to make her smile. But if someone else did this I'd be dreadfully jealous.

Sometimes she took me to see her grandparents, who lived in a small apartment in the 13th. The rooms smelled of age. Between the walls there was only silence and time, marked by the unceasing movement of the old clock. The place often made me feel dizzy. Sarah's grandmother was adorable. Her large breasts and thick arms made me think of my own mother's early embraces. When we'd come in for an afternoon snack a delicious smell of cake filled the hallway. I remember its caress on my tongue after I'd plunged a chunk into a mug of steaming hot chocolate.

As much as I liked the grandmother, I couldn't stand the grandfather. He was a dry, tall, hideous

43

type. His laugh was unbearable. During dinner he'd make disgusting noises as he swallowed his soup.

Sarah's grandparents had effectively withdrawn from the world. They asked for nothing, they simply wanted their granddaughter to be happy. Sarah was everything for them. But she regarded them as the people who'd destroyed her mother's life. I was often shocked by the way she spoke about them. She said she hated them, that it was all their fault, that neither she nor her mother had ever loved them. The only reason her mother ever came to visit them was because she owed them money.

I envied every facet of Sarah's personality. But I wasn't jealous of her. I admired her. She reassured me, she made me love life, she told me she adored me. Little by little a need grew within me that was to become stronger and stronger over the years: the need to have her there, next to me, to prove to myself that I had a place in her life. I simply couldn't imagine not being her best friend any more. I would have died just to hear her repeat that I was her number one.

In August we each went on our separate family holidays. Sarah went to Vendée with her mother and grandparents while I headed for Provence with my family. I sat on the terrace of the apartment and wrote her a letter every day. I told her all about my days spent tanning by the pool, the long, cool, dark evenings, my walks over the rocky hillsides, the little markets in the villages. I tried to include every detail, and in return I hoped to find dozens of letters from Vendée when I got back home.

The truth was that I was bored. I felt like I was nothing when she wasn't around. My friends from the previous summer were there, but I chose not to see them. I couldn't wait for the holidays to end. Somewhere inside me a secret promise had been made to belong to her and her alone.

The summer drew to a close. I returned home excited by the prospect of the letters that awaited me. A pile of mail had built up since our departure a fortnight earlier, but for me there was just a single postcard:

> Greetings to all from Vendée. Having a great time. Looking forward to seeing you in September. Love, Sarah and family.

And that was it.

I read the card again and again. But the message remained cold and hurtful.

It confirmed my fear that Sarah would have forgotten me by the end of the summer. It'd been too good, and too fragile, to last. She obviously had better things to do than be friends with a girl as useless and dull as me. I got the picture. I faced up to the fact that our beautiful friendship was over.

Playing

I didn't dare call her. Picking up the phone, dialling her number, confronting the sound of her voice – the very idea terrorised me. I dreaded her reaction. I knew her too well. I knew how she could use her authority and her quick wit to crush those who crossed her. And I knew, too, that one day she would turn on me.

The morning of the first day back at school I woke up with fear in my belly. How I wished I could avoid having to live through that day. We stood by the gates of Chopin and watched her make her majestic entrée. Her eyes were sparkling with mischief and an enigmatic smile played on her lips as she joined our group. She looked dangerous. I noticed that she was taller and thinner than when I'd last seen her. She was no longer a child. Her body had matured. Her features were finer now. She wore make-up, regardless of her professed hatred of it just two months earlier. Her hair shook as she moved her head in a show of indifference.

There was something indefinable about her. Something almost contemptuous. I felt fear as I watched her.

She barely looked at me. Or did I avoid her eye? She acted as though nothing could touch her. Just like a year earlier when she'd made her first appearance at Chopin, everyone almost instinctively stopped to listen when she started talking. She talked about her summer, her holiday on the Atlantic coast where she'd met a fabulous boy, where she'd spent an unforgettable August and experienced so many new things. She hadn't bothered to share any of this with me.

I couldn't stop myself staring at her in class. My eyes never left her impassive, almost hard face. When she spotted me she didn't flinch, she made as though I wasn't there. I could guess her thoughts. She knew what I was feeling, she knew I was watching her. She had it all worked out.

After class she made sure it was me who approached her.

She didn't let it show, but I knew she was enjoying this little victory. I felt more and more uneasy with every word I spoke. I was ridiculous – except that now me being ridiculous didn't make her laugh any more.

It was me who did all the talking, who asked the questions. I couldn't think of what to say, I repeated myself, I mumbled. All she did was reply to my questions with her usual arrogance. She

47

didn't even look at me. This was not the same Sarah I'd said goodbye to at the start of the holidays. Her reassuring words, the way she'd seemed captivated by me, it was all gone, everything that had authenticated my existence.

'So you had a good holiday? I got your card, that was nice, thanks. My parents appreciated it too. I hear you met a boy in Vendée. You didn't mention him . . .'

'Yeah, I went out with him. No big deal.'

'Did you get my letters? I wrote you dozens from Provence.'

'Yeah, I got a few. I haven't opened them yet. I haven't got much time at the moment. Listen, I've got to go, I'm going to have lunch in town with a friend.'

She ran off to join another girl from our class, a stuck-up cow that, last year, she'd said she couldn't stand. The two of them were laughing their heads off. Sarah was the clear winner in this sadistic new game whose rules she'd just revealed to me. I felt her provocation like a punch in the face.

I couldn't explain her attitude and yet it was as though I'd been expecting it from the start. Sarah was one of those people who, no matter what you do, always manage to remain superior. Even last year I'd seen this. The difference was that back then even she wasn't yet aware of it. But in the space of one summer, a couple of months in which she'd grown up, she'd realised that she was made to dominate others. The only role for a girl like me was one of submission.

We acted like we'd never been friends. The game lasted till the end of the autumn. When our paths crossed at school we were like strangers. We were waiting to see who could hold out the longest.

I spent my days idling, hanging about with whoever was available in smoky cafés full of gangs of boring kids. I'd dyed my hair raven black and wore only dark clothes. I looked a mess. I chain-smoked. Even in the middle of a group I was alone. Other people held no interest for me if Sarah wasn't there. Her absence tortured me, crushed me.

I observed her in class, in the yard, by the school gates, in the canteen, with her friends, laughing, talking, spurning my gaze. She seemed even more brilliant than before. I didn't know where I was. I made up all sorts of excuses to get my parents to let me go out. I started hanging out with a bad crowd. My school results suffered but I didn't care. As for Sarah, she had everything. Popularity, a really cool boyfriend, tons of friends, great marks. People swarmed around her. I hated them so much I wanted to kill them, I hated them because they could touch her, they could get her attention as once I'd been able to. Her life was glamorous while I remained stuck in an aimless, troubled, adolescent rut. She lived in the light. I was dying in the dark.

I would have given anything to have her back with me, and with me alone, just like before. Her absence made my days hell. The lump in my throat had made a comeback. I told myself that perhaps, as had happened last winter, Sarah would come to the rescue. Our friendship would be reborn as though there had never been any estrangement. The memory of the days and nights I'd spent with her gave me great pain. I was exhausted by the challenge she presented. I'd get up each morning and feel the weight of the world on my shoulders and wonder where I'd find the strength to get through the day. My aim was not to win. I simply wanted to hold on, I wanted her to come to me, I couldn't make the first move. Sarah had become an obsession. She dominated my life to such an extent that she drained it of all its points of reference, its past, my honour, my freedom.

She was winning, and there was nothing I could do about it. Drained of energy and of hope, I felt I had to disappear.

I ran away. I knew I'd be back in a few hours, long enough to calm down and to give my parents a good shock. It was October, it was cold. Night had fallen, I was walking down the road, alone, with no idea where I was going. I'd just had a huge fight with my parents, the worst so far, after they'd found cigarettes and lumps of hash in my room. I'd screamed and flung things at the wall. It was my pain that was screaming, my revolt. Everything came out. I told them, without really meaning to, that the 'accident' I'd had the year before wasn't an accident, and that it was their fault. They didn't believe me.

And then I packed my bag as they stood watching in disbelief. I waited for them to slam the door of my room behind them and then climbed out the window. I was cold. I smoked my last cigarettes to warm up. I walked, I didn't cry, I was trembling but calm, I simply headed for the horizon. I watched the white and yellow headlights of the cars pass me and fade into the distance. I walked on.

A car pulled over. I thought maybe it could take me somewhere, anywhere. I jumped in without a second thought. When I'd put on my safety belt and the car had driven off I turned to look at the driver. It was Martine, Sarah's mother. Sarah was in the back seat.

Once again I had lost, miserably.

I started crying.

No one spoke. I waited. The little Peugeot 106 stopped in front of my building. My mother was standing at the entrance, wrapped up in a shawl. I'd been set up. I got out of the car and walked over to her, my head down. I was ashamed. I knew she wouldn't hit me. My father would take care of that when he got home. Maman said nothing, she just stared at me. Sarah and her mother sat in the car and watched. It was their silence that I found the hardest thing to bear. I could see Sarah secretly rejoicing at this humiliation. 'You've won again, I hope you're pleased,' I thought.

When I realised my mother was waiting for me to make the first move I rushed into the building, unable to bear the silence any longer. I ran up to the apartment and went straight to my room. I wanted to lock myself in but they'd taken the key. I closed the door and fell onto the bed. I didn't cry. I waited for Sarah to come, I watched for the door to open. I feared that moment more than my father's blows or my mother's shouts.

I heard her approach. I felt her sit down beside me on the bed where I lay with my head buried in my hands. Suddenly her voice broke the silence. I can't remember what exactly she said. Reproaches, probably. My tears suffocated me. I heard her say again and again: 'Look at me when I'm talking to you!'

I just couldn't. I was too cowardly. I could only listen, I was paralysed by fear and shame.

'Charlene, look at what you've become! You've been running around with God knows who and now you're into drugs! What's happening to you? Are you enjoying ruining your life? Is that it? You like seeing others suffer because of you? You've really screwed up since school started. You don't bother calling me during the holidays and then when we get back to school you act like I don't exist. I thought you were better than that. You've really disappointed me. After all I've done for you.

Who came to see you in hospital after you tried to kill yourself? Who helped you get back on your feet? It was me, *your best friend*. And look where we've got to! I thought you'd understood. But you've proved me wrong. You've been running away from me. I suppose it's me who's going to have to sort you out again. What am I to do with you, Charlene? Tell me.'

Every word she said, every intonation, every vibration of her voice resonated in my chest. I trembled. My throat contracted, I was suffocating. It was the taste of suffering. I was suffering because I had disappointed Sarah, because she was angry with me, because I was no longer worthy of her. I was lost.

I wanted to tell her how much I hurt, that it was her fault too, that she had ruthlessly dropped me. But the words stuck in my throat. I could think only of the mistakes I'd made. I'd caused grief for so many people. I wanted to atone for my sins. I hated myself. It was the shame that was the worst. The helplessness. I was incapable of defending myself in the face of Sarah's crushing authority. After all, what she said must be right: I was worthless. I had the strength only to beg her to forgive me, to tell her I wanted her to be my best friend again, like she was before. I swore I wouldn't mess up again. I'd put a stop to my deviant behaviour, to the bad company, to my childishness. I beseeched her to give me one last chance. I'd have given my life to be her friend again. For her to make me feel, once again, that I had the right to be *someone*.

She gave me that chance. She wiped the slate clean.

From that moment on she held my life in her hands.

Nothing was ever the same again.

Everything seemed beyond me. My life felt like it was slipping between my hands like grains of sand. It was aimless, as in a void. I let myself be guided by just one thing, one voice: Sarah's. The fear of losing her again, the fear of not being worthy of her gnawed at me to the point where I could envisage only one thing. And that was giving myself to her entirely, body and soul, making my life her possession.

Sarah had put together a radical plan to make me become the person she wanted me to be. She ignored me. I had to carry on without the friendly gaze, the smiles, the compliments that once had given me confidence in myself. It was tough, but it was, after all, what I deserved. How could I refuse? Wasn't I lucky to be considered her best friend? To remain so I had only to obey her.

Nothing remained of our friendship. The fleeting moments of happiness, the mad laughter, the daring games of last year were all gone. Sarah was growing up, much faster than me. I was still a child, imprisoned in my dreams, in my revolt. I felt like I was just beginning to live, while Sarah was asking me to become an adult. I was all at sea, lost, unable to haul myself up to her level.

Her new friends never really accepted me in their group. Sarah made sure of that. I followed her everywhere, but all my efforts were in vain since she took great pleasure in ignoring me. She lived her life at great speed, played adult games, flaunted herself on the arms of boys much older than her, played confidante to every Tom, Dick and Harry. I hadn't the strength to keep up with her. I was still stuck in the past, I dreamt of finding the old Sarah again, sometimes I'd even pretend that nothing had changed.

Like a fool I waited and I hoped. Sarah terrorised me. Her face had become disdainful and proud. She smoked and I imitated her to try and appear more grown-up. She flirted with boys, so I pretended I was interested too. But in fact seeing her in a boy's arms was of more interest to me than my own conquests. I lived vicariously. Nothing could make me see sense.

My obsession grew. I was like an infection or a cancer. You don't know it's in you until the moment it starts to cause you pain.

There was this shrill little voice inside me, plaguing me. It reminded me of Sarah's existence at every moment.

'Look at her, Charlene. See how she ignores you.

She does it so well. She makes you invisible and at the same time she tortures you, she gobbles you up, she kills you. She acts like she can't see you, but she knows you're looking at her. She waits for you to be alone to say things that'll give you hope. Then she'll criticise you when other people are around. But never forget that without others she's nothing. That without *you* she's nothing.'

'What're you saying? I expect nothing from Sarah, she's my best friend. You're wrong, I know she likes me.'

'You're the one who's wrong. Just watch her and you'll see what she's up to. She's hiding lots of things from you. Follow her, spy on her, don't let her out of your sight. Watch everything she does.'

'Stop! You're mad! Leave me alone!'

That summer I pestered my parents for weeks to get them to take their holidays in the Camargue. Once they'd said yes I called Sarah one evening in a state of great excitement to tell her that she could come along with us. I knew she'd like that. I remember one day way back at the start of our friendship we'd been chatting in her living room and she'd taken an old postcard out of a drawer in the sideboard. It showed a landscape of rice fields stretched out in a fading light. She said she'd been sent the card by her mother when she was five and living with her grandparents. It was the first time she'd heard from her. She wrote that one day she'd take Sarah to see the Camargue. Sarah had been so delighted that she'd kept the card close to her ever since. Her mother had never kept the promise. Now Sarah was about to fulfil a childhood dream thanks to me.

The place we were staying in was a few kilometres from Arles, near the start of the Camargue marshes. It stretched out over several hectares, with dozens of little bungalows with pastel walls and red slate roofs dotted around landscaped gardens. In the distance you could see the dark green stalks of rice plants growing in abandoned paddy-fields. Our room was tiny and suffocating, and the only furniture was a set of bunk beds. The view from our window was of a windswept plain. We would often lie at night on the upper bunk and admire the fiery dusk that stretched out over the shapeless horizon.

The colour of the sky over the Camargue is like nowhere else in the world. It's a subdued, metallic white, slightly acid, a little burnished. It's as though two immense veils had been stretched out over each other, like a giant mosquito net, and above this net hovers a sun that changes from white to red over the course of the day. The burnt colour of Sarah's eyes matched that of the sky.

The heat was oppressive. Mosquitoes assailed us. The sun burnt our skin. After each exhausting, painful, stifling day came the night, warm and dense and strangely calm. From our terrace we heard the murmur of the crickets fade to give way to the brief, sonorous croaking of frogs.

Trapped by the heat, we'd spend hours stretched out on our beds trying to cool down with the help of the fan. Sarah would talk about her problems, her hopes, the future she'd worked out for herself. And I would listen, absorbed. Her determination fascinated me. I didn't know how to reply to her. I wanted to talk, I wanted Sarah to take her turn at listening, I wanted to get a dialogue going. But I wasn't able.

Sometimes I did manage to talk about myself. But I didn't have a lot to say. Sarah already knew all about my life, about my family, whom she now adored, my few 'friends' who were really her friends, my secrets, my little dreams. I could do nothing she didn't hear about. I'd long before stopped sharing with her my rare opinions about anything because I was afraid she'd disagree with them. I felt useless, dull. Sarah might have given me an identity two years previously, but in exchange she'd deprived me of a personality. But I hadn't been aware of that back then. A terrible idea crossed my mind at times, an idea that I could not come to terms with: she was my friend but I wasn't hers.

I watched her soften up first my parents, then my brother. Maman quickly fell for this charming girl who'd done so much for me. My father was captivated by her maturity, a maturity which he failed to see in his own daughter. Bastien found her exquisite. Her voice always dominated the conversation as we ate together on the terrace under giant sun umbrella. She spoke with the eloquence of an adult. Sometimes she'd disagree with my parents over political or moral issues and would argue it out with them till they finally came round to her point of view. She was an incredible talker, far too smart for a girl of fourteen. My parents listened to her words with astonishment and admiration. They soon came to adore Sarah and almost to consider her as part of the family. As for me, I loved her a lot more than I loved myself.

In the evening we'd talk again. Or, I should say, she'd talk. She even took the liberty of criticising the way my parents had brought me up.

'Do you want me to be frank with you, Charlene? You don't know how to take responsibility. You always need someone to hang on to, someone to give you moral support. I won't always be there to make decisions for you, you know. I've got my own life to live. Wake up a bit and decide that you're finally going to become a person in your own right. I've had enough of hanging about with someone who's got no personality of her own.'

'You're right. I'm sorry.'

'You're always sorry! That's about all you're good at. You've got no future. Poor little Charlene will always let people walk all over her. If you don't pull yourself together you'll end up no better than a slave to some slob of a man. My God, you're so stupid sometimes!'

I should never have listened to her, of course, but it was just too difficult to contradict her. I didn't know who I was any more. So I let myself be persuaded that my parents hadn't been strict enough with me, that I'd be more mature if they'd been tougher. I began to hate them for making me the way I was, for the sole reason that it didn't please Sarah.

Despite my pathological fear of horses I'd go along with her to the riding centre. We signed up for two treks through the marshes.

Sarah had found a friend. He was nineteen and he was called Matthieu. His father bred horses in the Camargue and he worked at the riding centre in the summer to help pay for his studies. He was an amazing rider. I can still picture the pair of them on their horses, side by side, talking as they rode. Matthieu was really good-looking. I used to look at him – secretly, of course, so as not to make Sarah suspicious. I saw his tanned skin, his firm body silhouetted against the sky, his grey eyes, and I was almost ashamed to be attracted by him. He spoke in the singsong accent of the south, and Sarah loved it. One evening he invited Sarah and me for a drink in the club bar and then took us for a midnight swim in the pool. I heard Sarah laugh as he whispered in her ear. I saw his eyes full of desire as they moved over her body. Later as Sarah and I walked home she couldn't shut up about him. I tried to tell her what she wanted to hear: that they were made for each other. In truth it enraged me to think of them being happy together.

So Sarah forgot about me once again.

In the evening she'd climb out of the bedroom window and not return till the small hours. Each night I hoped she'd come back and tell me it was over between them. But she never did. I could never sleep till she got back. When she did I'd close my eyes and pretend I was asleep. I'd listen to the rustling of the sheets as she slipped into bed, to her almost imperceptible breathing in the silence of the night. I wouldn't admit it to myself, but deep down I hated her.

It wasn't long till Matthieu started inviting Sarah out without me. She made it quite clear to me that they didn't want me around. I'd watch them from a distance, seething with hatred.

I was all alone, but that didn't bother Sarah. Nor did it bother me too much either. I'd found something to fill my empty days: I spied on her. I followed her from morning till night. I saw her every gesture, I heard almost every word, I observed everything she did. She didn't seem to mind. We'd made a tacit agreement – I'd leave her alone with her new friends and she'd tolerate my distant presence.

I'd get up at dawn and leave the room as quietly as possible so as not to wake her. I'd join my parents on the terrace for a breakfast during which we'd sit in an uneasy silence. I feared the moment when Sarah would finally appear, when I'd see her shadow moving behind the brown mosquito net. She'd kiss each of us on the cheek and join us at the table, smiling and laughing. As soon as my parents went off she'd shut up. She was waiting for me to beg her to tell what she'd got up to the night before. She'd adopt a scornful tone and, as though to fuel my frustration, tell me how she followed Matthieu to his room and made love with him in the half-light.

Sometimes I dreamed I'd been there in her place.

Our summer in the Camargue was over. We were due to leave the apartment at daybreak. I helped my parents load the car. In the distance I spotted a pair of silhouettes entwined in the first light of day. They were saying their goodbyes. Sarah walked slowly back towards us. She got into the car without a word. For the entire trip she sat and stared out at the landscapes that whizzed by. I heard her cry silently and that destroyed me. Nothing I said could comfort her. Each attempt was met with hostility. She didn't need me.

But, strangely, I was happy that it was all over. Because now I had Sarah all to myself again.

Submitting

It was not a happy autumn. We buried my grandfather at the start of October. I remember the foggy, damp morning, I remember the lump in my throat.

I arrived in front of the open coffin. My mother, her face devastated by the floods of tears that had poured down it since the death, held me by the arm and told me not to look. I looked. I looked at the dead man's face and it made me feel dizzy. I went and vomited behind the funeral parlour. I hadn't the strength to cry.

During the meal after the funeral I looked at them one by one, I studied them, as though I was seeing for the first time their terrible insignificance. They disgusted me. I pitied their stupidity, despised the insouciance and inanity of their pathetic lives. My family was no more than a squalid bunch of strangers to me.

Yet they hadn't changed. I had simply realised, after fifteen years of living with my parents, just how ridiculous they were. They'd both aged terribly, my mother from moaning non-stop with the sole aim of finding an obliging pair of arms into which she could throw herself, and my father, ever stoic, silent and tortured, from years of overwork that had destroyed everything around him. My paternal grandparents, for their part, had remained cloistered in their little world to protect themselves from any possible danger and now their lives consisted of waiting morosely for death.

They were all afraid. Their tiny lives were hemmed in by their need for security, by their selfishness. They knew nothing. They each tried to talk louder than the others around the dinner table, they spent their time disputing other people's ideas, but they had none of their own. Who were they? Where was my place in all this? Did they have even an inkling of how pathetic their lives were? They were prisoners of their own selves, how could they ever understand the hatred that seethed within me, this insignificant little person in their midst?

I walked out in the middle of the meal. On the veranda I found a cigarette that'd been lit and stubbed out after a few drags. I took it and slipped into the garage. I sat down on the cold concrete floor, my back against the car. The smell of petrol added to my feeling of faintness. I lit the cigarette. Its smoke was bitter, oppressive. I spat on the ground and stamped out the cigarette. I sat there in the dark, staring at a line of light that sneaked in through the window.

When I left the garage I realised that no one had even noticed I'd been gone.

Now that I'd become aware of what made me different from this family of mine and this world I lived in, there was just one thing I wanted to be close to, and that thing was Sarah.

I decided I'd give her everything from now on. I'd put more into our relationship. I loved her more than my own family, more than myself, more than life itself. I couldn't say why I loved her so much. It was not a love that brought happiness. On the contrary. To love too much, to love so much that your love becomes hatred, is to sacrifice your honour, to lose your liberty, to damage yourself. The love I had for Sarah was a perverse passion, painful, fierce.

Each morning after the alarm brutally ended my sleep I'd climb wearily out of bed and throw some ice-cold water on my face. Then I'd stand in front of the mirror to examine my nakedness in the shifting light. I told myself the same thing every day, it was like a mantra, I began chanting it the moment I opened my eyes, I chanted it as I made my way to school and again at night when I was in bed. My nights were sleepless, my head buzzing with always the same words: 'Be careful of your every word, every single thing you do when Sarah is around. One cock-up and you could lose her for good.'

I lived in the shadows. I survived only in the hope of winning Sarah's love. I hated my life. But I was too obsessed to be really aware of this.

I suffered Sarah, her looks, her reproaches, her silences, her absences. I had only to keep my mouth shut, to endure, to satisfy her. I thought that by lowering my eyes and biting my lip every time she'd make some unpleasant remark about me I could eventually win back her friendship. I wanted her to take me, to dominate me, to guide me. I was totally incapable without her. I was ready to give her everything, even my own death if that was what she wanted. I wanted to be her slave.

'Shut up, Charlene. I'm getting really pissed off with your whining and your childishness. You're boring me. Don't do anything. Don't think anything. Don't live. Just be happy being mine.'

It was awful. But admitting this would have meant admitting defeat. The only way out was silence. Besides, I knew I'd never be able to stand up to her. Another person would doubtless have fought back. But not me. My sole ambition was for everything to be like it was before, to savour again the friendship that we once shared. I thought that submitting to her was the way to win her esteem.

I could easily have decided to leave her, not to be her friend any longer. There was nothing making me stay. I was still free to live my life. But I never really considered this an option. I didn't take the time to imagine my life without her, without someone to hang on to. I refused to move on, to move away from the whirlwind that held me captive. So I let myself go. I was already dead.

66

One day shortly after the funeral I was walking in town, head down, not paying attention to where I was going, when a hand gently took hold of my wrist and shook me out of my thoughts. I looked up and found myself face to face with a girl about my own age, very tall and very skinny, smiling at me. I furtively looked at her before reacting. She was wearing an oversized sleeveless T-shirt and a pair of trousers that floated lightly around her legs. Her blonde hair was cut in a bob and framed a wan, emaciated face. Her eyes shone. They seemed to take up most of her face. 'You don't remember me, do you?' she said as I looked at her in silence.

Of course I knew who she was. I tried to smile and then I took her in my arms, hoping to find the Vanessa of my childhood. But all I found was a frail body that felt like it was ready to fall apart if I made a false move.

We went to a tea room. I devoured a *millefeuille* and watched her push her cake around the plate.

We talked for two hours, it was almost as though we'd never been apart. What was she doing with herself these days, what had brought her to Paris?

'Actually, I've been in hospital for the last month. I just got out today.'

Then she lowered her big eyes and said: 'I'm anorexic. I suppose you guessed that.'

She told me about her illness, the thirty-five kilos she weighed, the two years she'd spent fighting against her own body, the various hospitals she'd

67

been to, the treatment, the pressure the doctors put on her, how she'd nearly died.

'You know, I always thought we'd run into each other again some day. I thought about you a lot, especially when I was in hospital.'

I noticed that her fingers were playing with the pendant she wore around her neck, the one with the little blue ballerina that I'd given her six years earlier.

She asked me what I was up to. I replied: 'Not much, to be honest.' She said I'd changed a lot, that she hadn't imagined me like this, that I didn't seem as happy as I used to be. I burst into tears and told her everything. From the start, my suffering, my own personal hell. Despite the years that separated us, I let it all come out, even at the risk that she'd walk out on me and say I was mad. But she didn't walk out. When I'd finished speaking she simply placed her hand on mine and said: 'I don't know how to help you, but I would if I could. I'm there for you. I know what it's like to think you're mad. I know all about obsession. I've been through that just like you. But wherever you are, I'll be there for you. Never forget that nothing can separate us, Charlene, nothing. That was the promise we made, do you remember?'

And now it was her turn to take me in her arms, and it was me who suddenly felt fragile.

She gave me her number and her new address. I never contacted her. I just didn't have the strength to. I lost trace of Vanessa after that autumn afternoon. But one day, when I was in prison, I got a letter from her. She wrote that she was better. She was studying psychology, like she'd always wanted to. She didn't mention the murder. She simply wrote, at the end of the letter, that she'd always be my friend, whatever happened. And she signed it: 'Your little blue angel.'

I wouldn't know how to define obsession. I think you just have it inside you. It can be sparked by the slightest thing. It creeps into you, it slowly attacks every part of your being. It is cunning and manipulative, it passes itself off as your friend but never fails to betray you. Suffering is merely a side-effect. When you go mad you don't notice because it doesn't hurt. The most painful part is when the madness is over.

Martine invited me to spend New Year with her and Sarah in a chalet they'd rented along with some other families. These were friends of hers, old hippy types who met up at the same time every year. I accepted the invitation. So off I went with the pair of them, knowing perfectly well I was going to suffer.

It was a freezing cold night when the little black Peugeot 106 finally turned off the motorway. The wheels crunched over the gravel as the car came to a halt. Through the strange silence of this forgotten snow-covered place, voices, laughter, a few notes from a piano, and light emerged from the chalet, like a sign of life in the middle of a desert. I followed Sarah inside, dragging behind me the luggage she'd instructed me to carry.

There was a party atmosphere, everyone knew

each other. They greeted us and embraced Martine and Sarah, who, as usual, was the centre of attention. I stood there, not knowing what else to do. What did Sarah want me to do? To take part in things or to stay in the background? I was ridiculous. I looked over the place. On one side was the kitchen, all in metal, on the other the dining room with a big oak table in the middle, long enough to host the thirty-odd guests and already set for dinner. Between these two rooms was the living room, decorated in the local Alpine style. A broad staircase led off from the entrance up to the bedrooms.

Sarah's voice rose above the hubbub. She turned to me, but without really looking at me, and said I was Charlie, her 'best friend', a sort of pet to keep her company during the short holiday. I nodded at the guests' smiles and then Sarah took over again.

I followed her upstairs to the room reserved for the young people. We went in. Four girls were stretched out on their beds, chattering away and passing around photos of their boyfriends. They were roughly our age. Their conversation stopped when they saw us. Sarah gave a cry of delight and rushed towards them. There was much embracing and wild laughter. They already formed a little clan from which I was excluded. I stood sheepishly in the doorway and watched them while I waited for Sarah to tell me what to do. Sarah had, of course, forgotten about me. I knew her too well not to realise that she'd planned the whole thing from the start.

Her voice shook me out of my torpor. Her words were like hammer blows: 'What're you doing standing there like an idiot? Go and do something useful like helping mum unpack the car. I've got other things to do.'

There was a long silence. The other girls had stopped talking and were looking at me inquisitively. They were wondering why I let Sarah talk to me like that, why I obeyed her.

So. Sarah had imposed her authority on me in front of the girls. She'd shown yet again that she had all the power and my role was to submit.

When I woke up the next morning I was alone in the room. The others hadn't bothered to call me to go and join them for breakfast. I wearily headed for the dining room. My head was heavy and sore from lack of sleep. The night had been short. I'd spent a lot of it lying on the beds with the others, listening to them laugh and talk and tell each other about their latest amorous adventures while they stuffed themselves with sweets and smoked packets of Marlboro pinched from the storeroom. I stayed because there was nowhere else to go. I'd soon lost the thread of the conversation. Sometimes they turned to me, curious no doubt, and asked me questions about myself, what my ambitions were, did I have a boyfriend, did I – in short – have anything at all to say for myself? Since I didn't, Sarah stepped in for me: 'Her, a boyfriend? You must be joking! She's never been out with anyone. But then, Charlene, what boy with an ounce of sense would want a vegetable like you?' And she laughed. But she was the only one who found it funny. The others were silent. They stared at me, embarrassed. Sarah, seeing that my pathetic look had touched them, took up the conversation where it had left off and soon everyone forgot about the incident. It was really late by the time they went to sleep. I'd gone to bed a little before the others but had remained awake. Sarah's voice obsessed me. When she finally went to bed the sound of her breathing kept me awake.

In the morning all sorts of sounds were coming from the dining room – voices, laughter, children's squeals, the clinking of spoons against crockery and the whistling of the kettle as a backdrop to it all. The smell of hot coffee, steaming chocolate and fresh bread straight from the bakery titillated my still-sleepy senses.

I went and sat down by the other girls and said a half-hearted good morning to them. I began to eat my cereal, my eyes fixed on the bottom of the bowl. A voice called out my name. It belonged to Laetitia, one of Sarah's friends. She looked at me in a strangely reassuring sort of way as she waited for my response.

'Sorry . . . What did you say?'

'I asked was Sarah really your best friend.'

I took a quick look around the table. Sarah and the others had already left. I put my head down again and said in a single breath, as though it was something I'd learnt off by heart: 'Of course she's my best friend.

We've known each other since second year. She's always been there for me, even in the most difficult moments. We share everything, our secrets, our joys, our dreams. Sarah's fantastic, I owe her so much. In fact, I owe her everything. She got me out of some very difficult situations. I don't know what I'd have done without her. She's brought me so much happiness. I'm so grateful, I'd do anything for her. We're like sisters, her and me, like blood sisters.'

There was a long silence. I didn't know why I told her all that. I knew what she was going to say: 'But you saw the way she spoke to you last night? Why do you put up with that?'

'She's my best friend.'

'And that gives her the right to treat you like that?'

'Yes.'

'I don't get it. You're weird.'

I didn't reply.

'Anyway, I didn't think Sarah was like that. I can tell you it shocked us, the way she slagged you off last night in front of us all. You shouldn't let her get away with it. She's a little bitch, you know.'

I shrugged my shoulders and she went off. I sat there for a few moments, my eyes riveted on my empty cereal bowl. A violent, sickly joy had taken hold of me. The words 'she's a little bitch' gave me a deep feeling of satisfaction.

Night had fallen. The grey blue of the mountains and

the midnight blue of the sky merged on the distant horizon. It was the last night of the year.

The New Year's Eve dinner had been going on for ages. There was no end in sight. The dining room was filled with smoke and there was so much noise. Voices drifted into each other to form a deafening racket. The meal, too heavy and too long, was making me feel sick. My head spun. The music, the people, the laughter, the insouciance all weighed on me.

Occasionally someone would deign to pay me a little attention, they'd ask me was I OK, was I having a good time? I'd reply. 'Yes, thanks' and then they'd forget about me again. They'd turn back to Sarah. She was talking about her future. First she'd do her *baccalauréat*, in which she would, of course, get top marks, and then she'd go on to be a brilliant student at the Hautes Etudes Commerciales in Paris. She saw herself as a ruthless businesswoman stomping on her besuited male competitors. Maybe she'd have a go at politics, everyone said she'd be great at playing the tub-thumping technocrat. She was born to dominate, to lead. By the age of thirty she'd be rich, she'd buy an old farmhouse in the Camargue where she'd breed horses, marry Matthieu and keep a tight rein on him while he obliged her with some offspring. Maybe when she was about a hundred she'd consider dying.

Everyone listened to her, they knew that her predictions were probably accurate. Later everyone started dancing, with Sarah leading the way. She wore an ankle-length, charcoal-grey dress. The material covered her slim figure like a light, flowing veil. As she moved in the shimmer of the disco lights that had been set up in the room it seemed that her dress and her skin were of the same material. The dress seemed barely to touch her skin and quivered with each of her movements. She'd left her hair down and her thick red curls swept back and forth over her shoulders. She danced furiously, tirelessly.

I was bored silly. I reckoned that if I knocked back a lot of booze and got pissed then Sarah and the others might notice me. I started drinking. Glasses of spirits, white wine, cherry liqueur, red wine, beer, it all went down the same way. I was enjoying losing control. I let myself slip slowly into an almost comatose sort of happiness. The more I drank the more I enjoyed myself, so I kept on drinking. And suddenly Sarah noticed.

I'd gone up to the bedroom with the other girls. I was making them laugh and I liked that. They were probably making fun of me, the silly girl who must've seemed so uptight to them. The only person not laughing was Sarah. She told me to stop.

'OK, Charlene. It's not funny any more.'

But I couldn't stop now that I was the centre of attention. I was delighted that Sarah was jealous, that I was ruining her party. I was a danger to her and that pleased me enormously. I was feeling good. I saw the girls laugh for me so I had to go on. One more drink, let's see what happens.

We went downstairs to the kitchen. I was hanging

on to Laetitia and we were both laughing like mad. Sarah walked ahead of us, furious.

Then I drank that one too many. Sarah snatched the beer bottle from my hands so brutally that it ended up in pieces on the tiles of the floor. I'd hardly had time to see the splinters of glass flying around my feet when I felt her palm slap my face with such force that I fell over. A long, abominably heavy silence followed the blow. I looked up at her, my eyes brimming with tears. She stood there, haughty, terrifying. She looked like she was going to kill me. And I, poor little weak, shameful, miserable me, I silently begged her forgiveness. Time had stopped, nobody moved. She grabbed my arm and pushed me into the store cupboard without a word, as though this were an entirely normal thing to do. I was like her slave. I made no effort to defend myself. I stayed on the ground and kept my eyes closed because the tears were burning them. I didn't try to stop her, she had to do what she had to do. The blows didn't really count for much, she knew that my shame was much more painful.

She shook me violently. I could feel her breath on me. She was hurting me, but it didn't matter, I knew in my heart that I'd been expecting this moment for years. I savoured each blow, each bruise. They didn't feel like punishments, they felt like victory, a sort of culmination.

Sarah's shouts resounded in my stunned eardrums. I could hear the sound but could barely understand the words she screamed as she struck me. 'You're pathetic, Charlene . . . What do you think this makes me look like now? You just can't be responsible, can you? I'm fed up with your bullshit . . . You disgust me.'

I let her lock me in the cupboard. Then she went off and left me alone in the dark, cold space. I slumped on the ground, my head resting on the freezing tiles. I'd closed my eyes, I'd stopped breathing. I heard Laetitia's voice on the other side of the door: 'Charlene, let me in! Charlene! We have to talk, come on, open up!'

She gave up after a few minutes. From the living room I heard midnight strike and the revellers cheer. I saw in the New Year in the cupboard, my head in the dust and my mind in a state of confusion. I waited, unable to think any more. I spent about three hours in there. When I finally decided to get up, the party was still going on. I noticed there was some blood on the ground and on my clothes. Sarah must have cut me. I slipped up to my room and went to bed. No one saw me.

It was the light of day that woke me. I thought maybe I was still dreaming. My head was heavy, my mouth dry. The acrid taste of blood was still on my lips. I felt dirty. A dull sound thumped inside my head. The first image that came to mind was that of Sarah. I remembered the nightmare I'd just had. I'd dreamed of a bitter fight between us. She wasn't even trying to hit me, but I was doing my best to kill her, I was driven by unspeakable rage. But my hands never reached her body. I wanted to scream but my throat refused, it all stayed blocked inside me. Then I woke up. I felt like I was suffocating, constricted by the rage that had consumed me during the night.

I looked around. The room was silent. The girls were still sleeping, their breath barely audible. I sat up and breathed in deeply, letting the air slowly fill my lungs. I went over to Laetitia's bed and whispered her name till she opened her eyes.

'Charlene? What's wrong? What time is it?'

'It's OK, everything's fine. It's early. Why isn't Sarah in her bed? Where did she sleep?'

'In her mother's room. She said she didn't want to wake up near you this morning.'

'Thanks. Go back to sleep now.'

I left the room and walked stealthily down the main corridor. Nobody was up yet. The chalet felt abandoned. I went to Martine's room and opened the door carefully so as not to make any noise. My feet slowly guided me towards Sarah's bed.

I crouched down to look at her. Even asleep she had the same scornful and cold look on her face. Even asleep she frightened me. For a moment I wanted to shatter her tranquillity with a scream. For an instant I hoped to see her lying dead before me. Then I heard a noise in the corridor and I got up and left.

When I got back home I half-heartedly wished my parents a happy New Year. I went and shut myself in my room and, just as when I was a child, closed the shutters so that I could be in total darkness. Alone in the dark, I felt safe.

I took out everything: photos, albums, diaries, letters, notebooks, souvenirs. In a single afternoon I reviewed my entire life, my past that I had tried so hard to bury. I saw that before Sarah I'd had a life, a happy childhood, an existence that belonged to me and me alone. I'd been happy. I'd been free.

Photos of me. Twelve years old: standing by the pool at sunset with my holiday friends, Vaucluse, summer '96. Ten years old: between my father and my mother, Bastien squatting in front of us, the guests in the background around the table, Christmas '94. Eight years old: in pyjamas, snuggled up under the covers, Vanessa lying on the bed beside me, no date. Five years old: a cheeky little tomboy sitting on Grandfather's lap, autumn '89. Two years old: a fine summer's day, a straw hat and a little stripy dress, taking my first steps, my hand in Maman's. Two days old: the maternity hospital, my mother holding me in her arms, my father standing next to us. They smile, they look emotional. The picture makes me cry.

I realised my life had not always been sordid. I'd been loved, perhaps I was still loved. For my parents, my brother, Vanessa and a few others I was a whole person, I was part of their lives and they of mine. I felt light-headed. The shock of this truth made me feel sick.

How could I have been so blind? I'd sought love and friendship. I thought I'd found it in Sarah. For almost two years I'd tried desperately to rekindle it. Sarah had destroyed everything, she'd driven me away from myself.

And there were some people who had loved me during all this time. In my blindness I hadn't been able to see that love.

Sarah's journey through my life had ravaged it. I was a weak being, tortured, scared, silent. Submissive. I had demeaned myself, I had lost my identity.

I looked at the photos spread across the floor and thought about my past. It was all so clear to me, it was not by chance that Sarah had used me the way she did. She knew from the start that I was weak and easily influenced. And she needed me as much as I needed her. Maybe she knew from the start that I was mad or could easily become so. Whatever the case, I had not opposed her, I'd accepted her rules, I'd indebted myself to her. At a certain point in my life, she'd given me confidence in myself and had become the only person with whom I had any real communication. From that moment the rest was unavoidable. I told myself that, after all, perhaps I wasn't the only one who was at fault in the whole affair. Maybe Sarah was as mad as I was, but destiny saw to it that once our paths crossed, I would come out the loser. For the first time, after years of blindness, I realised the contempt I could feel for the girl. For so long I'd taken my feelings to be fascination, but perhaps it is just a short step between hatred and passion.

I turned my eyes towards the mirror, the looking-glass that had so terrified me as a child, and there I saw a stranger. A girl, naked, squatting, her cheeks wet with tears, looked vacantly out at me. I couldn't bear the sight. I took the nearest thing to me, my bedside lamp, and flung it at the mirror. Then I picked it up and used it to hammer the frame till there was no glass left. The splinters made my hands bleed.

Loving and Being Loved

I realised that leaving Chopin to move on to the *lycée* was my only way out. I was ready to flee this life which Sarah had made into a hell. We would finally go our separate ways when we left Chopin, of this I was convinced. So it was with a sense of growing relief that I watched the approach of summer.

I was about to leave behind me four painful years. I hoped that I would start enjoying life again, that I would move beyond my dangerous liaison with Sarah. I would live again, without fear, without scorn, without shame.

I prepared myself for the rupture. It was like preparing for battle. Would I be able to survive without her? I tried to persuade myself that I would. I thought I'd be strong enough to be able to stand up to Sarah and say no when she asked me to go to the same *lycée* as her. I was wrong. I acted like a coward, I looked down at the ground and agreed.

In September I went to the Lycée Baudelaire and once again the gates of hell closed behind me.

It was the first day of school. I looked at the various groups of students hanging about in the street in front of the *lycée* and saw no one I knew. The immense school building terrified me. It was twenty, maybe thirty metres tall and stood on the edge of a large square lined with plane trees and benches. There were two courtyards, separated by a second building. The plaster on the walls was worn and dark and gave me a foretaste of the prison where I was to live years later.

I feel lost. I make my uncertain way into the classroom. I look over the rows of students. Sarah is there. I breathe a sigh of relief, for in truth this is what I wanted. She's sitting at the back of the class, looking at me, a mocking smile on her lips. I note that the other students are already stealing admiring glances at her.

Sarah had decided that I should no longer exist, at least temporarily. Of course, officially I was still her best friend. But on the first day of school I wasn't to let anyone know this. And for the next few weeks, months even, she pretended she didn't know me when we were in public. The game went on, we didn't look at each other, never spoke. She was having a good time, she laughed very loudly so that I could hear. She told her new friends everything about herself to show me that I was no longer her confidante. She knew I suffered much more from her lack of attention than from her reproaches or criticism.

She was not unaware that she was making me ill. It was torture, I was completely obsessed by her, I was close to madness. Her inhuman behaviour continued, and I knew exactly what she was thinking: 'Don't even bother begging, Charlene. I'm the stronger one. I'll go right to the end, I'm enjoying this.'

I spent my days on my own, spying on Sarah. She knew perfectly well I was watching her every move. I didn't want to miss anything she said, it was as though I were living in her shadow. I was no longer in control of myself, and my entire being was overwhelmed by a violence and an anger I'd never before known.

Rumours about me were rife: I was psychologically disturbed, deeply depressed, subject to mood swings and uncontrolled aggression. It didn't take me long to figure out that Sarah was behind these stories. She was the only one who knew that when I was thirteen I'd tried to end it all.

So for months I watched as the other students avoided me. I put up with their indifference, their questioning looks, their whispering behind my back. I frightened them. But in truth I didn't really care what they thought. Sarah was the only one who counted. She continued to provoke me, to make me look stupid. The others approved. All the secrets I'd shared with Sarah in the past now became material for sneers and rumours. I was appalled, but I was too alone and too powerless to do anything. Her betrayal was worse than her absence.

Unconsciously, slowly, I was already planning my revenge.

For a long time Maxime was no more than a neck that sat in front of me in French class. A long, straight, bare neck topped with a blond head with neatly cut hair and flanked by a pair of ears that stuck out a bit. He was very tall and very thin, and maybe a little too frail for a boy of sixteen.

We had displayed mutual indifference. He hung out with a group of boys that I found fairly childish. I couldn't have cared less about him, nor about the others, nor about myself.

But no. I'm not telling the truth. Maybe I always knew that he was different, that he was more mature than his friends. The rumours, the contempt, Sarah's influence in the class, he wasn't at all interested, he told me later. He secretly intrigued me. But at the time I was too caught up with Sarah to have time for him. We never spoke to each other and got no further than exchanging occasional furtive glances.

Until that morning in October.

It was raining. I still remember the smell of damp earth that filled the streets. I'd gone out in the middle of a storm that lashed the grey city.

I went into the little bookshop on the corner of the Rue des Haies. The silence there was in sharp contrast to the noise the torrential rain made outside. It was Saturday morning and the shop was deserted. I loved the hushed atmosphere, I could spend hours in there among all the books and the smell of dust and paper.

My father used to bring me here when I was little. While he browsed the history shelves, I discovered the smooth, glossy feel of paper, the smell of book covers both new and old, the rustling sound the pages make when you turn them one by one. It was in this little bookshop that I learnt the pleasure of words, of letters, of paper, their taste, their smells, their caresses.

I'd gone in there that morning because there was something I needed to know. I wanted to know if there had been other cases similar to mine, if I really was sick, and how I could get over this. Was there after all some explanation for what I was going through?

I went straight to the shelves that lined the back of the shop under the word Psychology. I scanned the books there, the names of the authors, the dates of publication, the editions, the titles, and then took out the ones that looked relevant. I leafed hurriedly through them, hoping to find an interesting passage. I'd heard about a recent biography that'd caused a scandal in the United States. It was the story of a young man condemned to death who recounted how he came to brutally murder his father and his two uncles.

A few shelves lower down I came across a book on fanaticism and on the murderous desires it can kindle. My eyes ran feverishly over the words, drinking them in

> Death constitutes the absolute . . . It is impossible to go beyond this frontier . . . One can no longer redefine oneself . . . It abolishes everything . . . It is a logical and ideal recourse . . . The limits of paroxysm . . . Culmination . . . Excess . . . Relief . . .

From another shelf I grabbed a Camus novel that we'd looked at briefly in French class: *The Outsider*. One of the passages seemed to be written especially for me. I was fascinated but I didn't know why:

> My whole being went tense and I tightened my grip on the gun. The trigger gave, I felt the underside of the polished butt . . . I shook off the sweat and the sun. I realised that I'd destroyed the balance of the day . . . And I fired four more times at a lifeless body and the bullets sank in without leaving a mark . . .
>
> As though this great outburst of anger had purged all my ills, killed all my hopes, I looked up at the mass of signs and stars in the night sky and laid myself open for the first time to the benign indifference of the world.

I read the passage several times. Meursault's fate was my fate. I suddenly realised that this was something glaringly obvious but which until then I'd never even suspected. When I finally looked up from the book, I spotted him. A few metres away from me, at the Modern Poetry section. Maxime. I stood there and stared at him. His face appeared frozen, his brows like two brown waves above his eyes, his mind focused on the book he held in his hands.

As soon as he moved he looked in my direction. I immediately looked down again at my book. For a few moments I pretended I hadn't noticed him and waited for him to make the first move, as I knew he would.

He said a shy hello.

I looked at him and pretended I was surprised to see him. He was smiling.

'What are you doing here? I didn't know you came to this bookshop.' he said after a brief, embarrassed silence.

I don't know what to say. He leans over towards me. He has this gentle, reassuring look on his face.

'What're you reading?'

'*The Outsider*. I've been meaning to buy it since we talked about it in class.'

'I love that book. The style is really spare but the story is really poignant. You must read it.'

'What are you going to buy?' I muttered, looking at the book he was holding.

'Well, I was thinking of getting this book of poetry. Jean Tardieu, don't know if you know him . . .'

'Vaguely. I didn't know you were into poetry.'

He looks down at the ground and smiles shyly. He's sweet.

'Uh, yeah, I am,' he says. 'Sometimes. If you want we can go somewhere and talk . . . What are you doing now?'

'I don't know, nothing really. I was thinking of going home. Why?'

'Er, if you like we could go and have a drink. I know a nice café near here.'

I didn't have the time to hesitate or to refuse.

I paid for my two books and we left the bookshop. I obviously didn't tell Maxime the real reason why I'd bought *A Psychological Study of Obsessional Murder*. The rain had eased. We walked in silence to a café on the corner of the Rue de l'Harmonie. We sat at a little table in a corner. He took off his dripping sailor's jacket and hung it over the back of his chair. I ordered a hot chocolate, he asked for an espresso, he insisted on paying. We sat there for a while without saying anything, looking out at the deserted street.

He lit a cigarette. I looked at his fingers, long and fine, delicate and fragile. His fingers were like he was. Sarah said you could figure out a person by looking at his hands. Her own were beautiful. Maxime had the hands of an artist, of a writer. I had always sensed a sophistication in him that the other boys lacked.

He smoked elegantly. Little clouds rose up around us. I looked at his finely-drawn lips, his very short and very straight nose with its almost invisible little nostrils. And those eyes, veiled by the lenses of the glasses that gave him, I must admit, a certain charm. At first I didn't want to return his looks. I would have to give too much away were I to look into his eyes. I was of course dying to get to know him better. But slowly.

He started talking. His voice was clear, soft and solemn. I hung on his every word. I immediately had the impression that I was in the presence of an exceptional person. Maxime fascinated me.

I listened to him tell me he wanted to be a doctor in a busy casualty department because he liked risk and the unexpected, he thrived on tension and challenge. He said he'd been living with his sister since his mother died a few years ago, he didn't say a word about his father. Little by little, I learned who he was. He said he was mad about sculpture and video games, he adored science fiction as much as he liked classic and contemporary literature – Zola, Steinbeck and Duras were his favourites. He was a fan of Rodin and Picasso, of Bob Marley and Chopin and Zinédine Zidane, he loved the psychedelia of Pink Floyd as much as he liked rhythm and blues. Then he said he couldn't stand the economics teacher and could I explain the last chemistry experiment we'd done because he hadn't a clue what it was about.

I liked him. He even managed to make me laugh. Nobody had been able to do that since Sarah. But the anxiety that is always with me snatched this pleasure from me. What if he found out? What if he could see me for what I really was? I didn't want to get involved. He was too perceptive not to realise what I was up to.

I don't know why Maxime decided to be my friend after that rainy autumn morning. After school, he'd take me to the café in the Rue de l'Harmonie. We'd sit at our usual table, he'd order his espresso and me my hot chocolate, we'd smoke entire packets of Camel cigarettes, whose heavy taste would make my head spin. He'd talk and I'd listen, absorbed. I had nothing to say. Whenever he asked me a question I'd give a really short answer so as not to give myself away. Our friendship was still too fragile to let him even glimpse the terrible secret that weighed on me.

We'd stay in the café until very late, sometimes until closing time. He always walked me home. We'd say goodbye at the door of my building and I'd watch him disappear into the night.

Sometimes he'd invite me to lunch at his place, the little apartment in the 14th where he lived with his sister, his brother-in-law and his two nephews. They were always really nice to me. During the meal they'd all listen, amused and affectionate, as Maxime talked tirelessly. He talked so much that he hardly touched his food. His attitude, his slight clumsiness, thoughtfulness, everything about him charmed me and, little by little, brought me back to normality.

The apartment was much too small for five people. I remember his tiny room in the attic, always in a mess. Dozens of posters covered the walls, mostly old film posters and black-and-white photos – almost all of his mother. Only the books on the shelves had been ordered according to their category. The first time he took me into his mysterious universe he threw open the window and said: 'Voilà. This is my world.' Below us the rooftops of Paris stretched out to the horizon. Maxime said it was the first time he'd brought a girl here. I smiled. Suddenly I felt less vulnerable. He was there, next to me, I was happy. Almost too happy.

He was becoming my friend and sometimes this was painful to admit. I had asked for nothing yet he sought to discover me, to tame me. But I was still not hoping for anything. My madness was enough for me. I needed no support, no love that did not come from Sarah.

But perhaps, deep inside me, I knew he was bringing me the help that I'd always needed.

A new Charlene slowly began to emerge. Sarah's absence became less and less painful. Maxime loved life and I let myself get swept up by his joy, I even began to share it with him.

Weeks went by. Then suddenly I lost control of the situation. Maybe I'd been fooling myself or maybe things somehow changed between us. I couldn't fall in love, no, not me. The voice deep inside me began to scream. No, it said, you belong to Sarah. To her alone, do you hear? Yet Maxime's presence had become an essential part of my life.

I was sixteen and had never been in love, had never known any affection other than what my parents or my rare friends had given me. I knew nothing about passion, not even what it was like to kiss someone. The idea of loving someone was inconceivable. Most of the girls in my class were no longer virgins. Certainly not Sarah. I was so jealous of the boys she flirted with, the boys who looked at her with desire in their eyes. All I ever got was the occasional pathetic wink. No one had ever loved me. And I felt incapable of giving my love to a boy. The very idea terrified me. Because the one time that I'd felt something for someone was for Sarah, and that had, over time, turned into this sickly obsession.

I must not love Maxime. Not him. Loving him would inevitably mean making him suffer. He already knew me too well. Perhaps he even knew that I was mad, that the rumours about me were not unfounded. Yet he had clearly decided to hold on to me, he wanted to know everything about me.

He said he could see right inside me. That he liked me, he found me interesting, that he was attracted to me. Silently I begged him to stop.

Already I was causing him pain. I refused to love him for fear that our relationship would become like the one I had with Sarah. The prospect filled me with fear.

I started saying no to his invitations for a drink after classes. I pretended my parents wouldn't let me because they said I had to study more – in fact, they didn't care what I got up to. I said no when he insisted I come for lunch with his family. I avoided looking him in the eye, I stopped paying attention to the talk that had previously captivated me. After a while I decided that Maxime should no longer exist for me. The truth was that I wanted to spare him. I was certain that he could be happy without me.

I took the metro one evening in November. It was very cold, night had fallen. When I got out at Emile-Zola station the chill was almost violent. I walked towards my apartment building. When I reached the front door I heard a faint voice behind me. 'Charlene! Wait, we've got to talk. Look at me, please.'

It was Maxime, standing in the glare of the streetlights. He was right beside me, staring impassively. The snow fell on his blond hair.

'Did you follow me?'

'Yes.'

'You shouldn't have. Leave me alone.'

'It was the only way I could make you listen to me.'

'All right, go on then. Talk.'

'I think it's you who needs to do the explaining.'

'What do you mean?'

'Don't play the innocent, Charlene. You've been hiding from me, you know that.'

'Don't know what you're talking about. I told you my parents are putting their foot down and . . .'

I stopped short. His eyes tore me apart. I wanted to scream at him to go, to disappear from my life. Instead I murmured into the silence of the night:

'It's best that you go home now. I'm in a hurry, I've got to go.'

'Charlene, what's going on?'

The truth was burning my lips. Maxime moved closer to me. He took hold of my arms.

'OK. Since you insist, I'll be frank with you. We can't be friends any more. It would only cause you grief. You don't deserve that. You've heard the rumours about me? Well, it's true that I tried to kill myself when I was thirteen. I'm not like the others, you know. I don't know why I'm telling you this. You should go, you shouldn't get close to a girl like me. I'm not the one for you, I'm not worthy of your friendship. You must have better things to do than waste your time with someone like me. Enjoy being sixteen, go and meet someone else, have a nice time, I beg you, Maxime. I care for you too much to let you . . .'

'Stop.'

He was now so close to me I could feel his breath. He folded me in his arms. I felt a little shudder in my stomach, but it was not fear. I let him kiss me, I let him press his body against mine.

It was an intense happiness, a happiness that grew stronger as the months passed. I'd never known anything like this. I was becoming a normal person. An ordinary teenager, like any teenager you might see in any school. I began to be able to put up with myself, to accept myself, almost to love myself. And I loved Maxime, without being obsessive. It was a love without hatred, it was the simplest thing in the world, it was just like what everyone else seemed to be able to do so easily.

I loved so much that I forgot Sarah. That I was no longer interested in her presence. That I no longer listened to the little voice inside me. That I thought I was finally cured.

I felt safe when he put his arms around me, I loved to breathe in the smell of his pullover when I walked around town with him, his hand in mine. Just being next to him, looking at his face and his hands, smelling his scent, observing the contours of his lips, all these little details made my happiness. I learned to laugh, to stop lowering my eyes when he looked at me, to let him whisper 'I love you' in my ear, to believe his words, his promises.

There you are. I think that's what it's about, loving someone.

Maxime said he'd like to meet my parents. I couldn't see the point. I'd never really confided in them, and the idea of introducing my boyfriend to them was embarrassing. They didn't know much about him, except that he was maybe something more than just a friend to me. But Maxime kept on about it so I gave in.

He arrived at seven o'clock. I opened the door to him and he kissed me on the cheek, perhaps because my parents were there. With a clumsy and slightly intimidated gesture, he handed my mother a bouquet of blue flowers and gave my father a bottle of Baume de Venise.

My parents liked him straight away. His simplicity, his frankness, his humour, his *joie de vivre* – everything that had seduced me charmed them. They must have been thinking that it was at least partly thanks to him that I'd changed so much over the past few months. Time seemed to stop at a certain point in the evening. They were all there, Maxime, my parents, Bastien, all the people I loved and who loved me. I realised I was happy.

At nine, when dinner was over, Maxime and I went out into the cold of the night. He said he thought my parents were really nice, my mother was charming and my father a laugh. He said he loved me. He didn't stop saying he loved me. We stopped briefly in the Café de l'Harmonie, our old haunt, and then continued walking through the deserted streets until we reached his place. He invited me in. I hesitated. Then I followed him, still holding his hand, up to his bedroom.

We could hear the patter of rain on the street outside. It was dark and I couldn't make out his face even though it was right next to mine. I breathed in the smell of the rain and the sweat of a body that called to me.

I let him. He was gentle, silent. I yielded to his clumsy gestures, to his trembling hands. When I knew it was the moment, that I was ready to abandon myself to him, I closed my eyes so that I wouldn't have to think.

'It's OK. I love you.'

The tenderness of his 'I love you' calmed my trembling even as I felt the pain slowly enter me and then grow dull. As our bodies sealed into one I listened to his heart thump and thought perhaps it might bring my own back to life.

When the lovemaking was over he switched on the light and lit a cigarette. I lay stretched out on the other side of the bed, with my back to him. I watched the rain through the window. We didn't speak. He rolled over next to me and asked me if I loved him. His skin was nice and warm. I felt his breath on mine and I trembled. He started talking. I didn't listen to what he said. There was a knot of apprehension in my stomach.

'There's something I have to tell you, Maxime.'

I turned to face him. The brightness of his face dazzled me. I muttered: 'Sometimes I kill the people I love.'

I burst into laughter, thinking he would do the same. But he didn't. I'd never seen such a look of fear on his face.

Losing the Game

For five months I believed in happiness. I believed in it passionately, hopefully, with conviction. I'd taken a liking to it, and I refused to consider that sooner or later this happiness might escape me.

In the end it wasn't the happiness that went away. It was me who fled.

During all the time that Maxime and I loved each other, I thought that the Sarah business was over. I'd managed to transfer my love to someone else. Someone who knew how to return it. But, in fact, it was far from over. The obsession had to re-emerge sooner or later. Such intense, tenacious pain, such folly could not disappear so easily.

Nor had Sarah, for her part, cast me out of her life. And she chose the best moment to take back from Maxime that which belonged to her.

She called to me one Friday in May as we were leaving school. I'd almost forgotten the sound of her voice.

'Hi, Charlene. So how are things?'

I gave her an incredulous look. She was walking quickly to keep up with me. Now it was her turn to look at me as though she had something to feel guilty about. It was the first time I'd ever seen her embarrassed. I was dumbfounded.

She asked me what I'd been up to all this time. 'You know, we've grown apart since you started going out with Maxime. It's not like it was before.' She said she was happy for me. 'You've really come out of yourself, Charlene. He's a good bloke. You deserve him, you really do.'

'As for me, well, I'm not doing too well at the moment. Maybe you heard that my grandmother died in January. Things have been tough for us since then – financially, I mean. We were fairly dependent on her. And have you noticed that people are snubbing me at school? Rumours. I've been getting all sorts of abuse, you know. It's not easy when you've got a reputation.'

'I know that, Sarah.'

Then she said she'd been thinking a lot about us, about our friendship. She was really sorry that things had turned out the way they did. She'd love to be able to confide in me, like before: 'Now I can see that it wasn't always easy between us. But that's in the past. We've both grown up a lot since then.'

Then she said this: 'I'm sorry, Charlene. For everything I did to you.'

Anyone else but me might have cried victory. I

should have looked my adversary in the eye for the first time, I should have walked away the victor of this struggle, my head held high, no regrets. But I didn't. I made the worst mistake I could possibly make. I plunged back in. I saw the sadness in her eyes, I felt sorry for her. I gave in, like a coward I sympathised, and thereby sealed for ever the pact with my madness. She suggested I sleep over at her place the following Saturday, just like when we were kids, to chat, to *be together again.*

'All right, Sarah. I'll come, I promise.'

So I ended up again in the little apartment in the 12th that I knew so well, with its heavy silences, its pale light, its unmistakable smell. Our secret whispers in the half-light of Sarah's room resumed as though they'd never stopped. I saw again the radiance of her laughter, the pain of her tears when she confided in me, the perfume of her hair next to my face when I woke in the morning, the clarity of her voice, her disconcerting glances, it all started again.

I wanted to believe in it. I convinced myself that Sarah had changed as much as I had. I thought we both wanted to get back to the friendship we had when we were thirteen, to forget the hatred that had torn us apart. I wanted to believe in it. And I did.

I told myself that all that had happened in the past wasn't really so bad. That from now on Sarah and I would be equal, that there was no winner and no loser. Now that I had Maxime and Sarah my happiness would be complete. Harmony had come into my life and I no longer had anything to worry about: I was cured.

The truth is that I couldn't see what was about to happen. Or rather that I chose not to see.

'What's wrong, Charlene? Where are you, tell me?'

Maxime's voice disturbed the calm. I pressed myself against him, we kissed. I didn't know how to answer. How could I console him? I hadn't the strength.

'Everything's fine, Maxime. Don't worry, everything's fine.'

'Charlene, please. Don't get mixed up with her again. You know what'll happen.'

'No. I swear, she's changed. She's not like she was before, she wants us to be friends again.'

'Sorry, but I just don't believe that. If I were you, I'd give that girl a very wide berth.'

'Leave me alone.'

I jumped off the bed. Without a word, I got dressed as he watched, disillusioned.

'I have to go. Sarah's waiting for me. We're going to a restaurant tonight with her mother. Bye.'

I give him a frosty kiss on the lips. I leave without having the time to reply to the 'I love you' that I hear behind me in the bedroom, like a last desperate cry.

No, I didn't see it coming.

I was once again part of Sarah's game. I believed all her promises, I let her reassure me. I listened to her sorrows, I took her in my arms to let her cry, and, naturally, I promised to help her as much as I could, I swore it in the name of our friendship. She managed to persuade me that it had all been my fault. I alone was responsible for her distress, she'd decided that this was the case and I must now plead guilty.

So, as I'd promised, I helped her. I took whatever I had from saving months of pocket money and from odd jobs and gave it to her mother to help her pay off her debts. Then I set about convincing all her old friends that Sarah really had changed, that she was a nice girl. I spent hours listening to her – time that I could have spent with Maxime. I gave her everything. All the love that I had, all my strength, whatever courage and goodwill I had left. All this simply to hear her say that I was still her best friend, the most important person in her life now and for ever.

I again began to watch her every movement, at first simply to reassure myself and to check that she was all right. But it soon became an obsession. Then it all started over again, she started to laugh again, she never told me where she now spent her evenings and weekends, she hung out with people older than her – I hated them – and she never bothered to invite me anywhere. I was transparent,

I was dead a second time now that she ignored me. Later, suddenly filled with some frantic desire, I took to calling her in the middle of the night just so that the sound of her voice could prove to me that she was at home and not out with her new friends. Whenever I was in her apartment I couldn't resist the temptation to steal objects belonging to her or to root in her drawers, because I thought she might be hiding things from me. She'd been able to reverse our roles in no time at all, and now it was me who needed her for reassurance, it was me who got down on my knees to beg for her attention.

When my eyes were finally opened, it was already too late. Sarah had used me, she'd used my support to get back on her feet. Deep down, she hadn't changed. I could've taken advantage of her moment of weakness to do something, to crush her, but I'd been impotent, I'd believed in her. When I was forced to admit my terrible failure, when I finally realised the extent of her treachery, I was again filled with hatred, a hatred now stronger and more painful than ever.

Everything changed radically after June. Summer had arrived, a fine summer with lots of sun. I stayed in my room most of the time, ignoring Maxime's frequent calls. I phoned Sarah every day but all I ever got was her voice on the answering machine. 'Hello, you're through to Sarah and Martine but we're not available at the moment. Please leave a message after the beep and we'll get back to you as soon as we can. Thanks. Bye.' When the signal came I'd remain silent. But I'd stay on the line until the allotted time for the message was over and the long, repeated tones rang in my ear.

I spent most of my time looking for her, calling her, dropping into her apartment, sending her letters, whatever. I wrote about whatever I thought might interest her. I'd tell her about anything, about the most banal little incident in my little life, or, unable to think of anything to pad out my paragraphs, I'd invent stuff. I wondered what she might be doing, where she was and with whom, if she was happy, if she was thinking about me and if she missed me. Days and weeks went by without a word from her. I checked my letterbox every day and found only letters from Maxime that I hadn't the courage to open. I told myself that there must be a problem with the post, that Sarah must have been sending her letters to the wrong address. It was the only explanation I could find. Living without her presence was unbearable for me. I was obsessed. But I knew she'd come back to me. I knew that she hadn't completely abandoned me, that sooner or later we would be one again.

The voice returned. I started talking to myself again.

'What do you want, for God's sake? Can't you leave me alone once and for all and let me live my life?'

'Shut up. It's all your own fault. It's too late now to go back.'

'What exactly do you want? Just what do you hope to get from harassing me like this?'

'I just want you to give in. Once you've done what I ask it will all be different, that I can promise you. I won't bother you again. You can live your life as you please, I won't be there to bother you any more.'

'Tell me what I need to do to make you go away.'

'I want to know if Sarah is lying to me. I'm sure she's hiding something. I want you to spy on her, follow her, watch her until she gives in. You have to be stronger than her, so that it's her who begs for forgiveness. Once you're sure that she belongs to you, that you have the upper hand, once you've made her pay for everything she made us suffer, then I'll go away.'

'You swear?'

'I swear.'

One morning in July I dialled Sarah's number. I counted three or four ringing tones and then, at the moment when the recorded message should have started, I heard, as though in a dream, her voice. I started trembling and thought about hanging up. But she'd caught me off guard.

'Charlene, I know it's you.'

'...'

'Charlene?'

'Did you get my letters?'

'And all the anonymous phone calls too. Your messages on the machine. There were hundreds of them. Looks like all you did over the holidays was leave me messages. I nearly called the police, you know. But then when I figured out it could only be you I reckoned we had to sort it out between ourselves.'

'You were never there . . . I didn't know where you were.'

'I was in the south with my friends. We went on a little adventure. It was fantastic, if you really must know. Of course, I couldn't take you along. As you know, my friends aren't necessarily yours, and these particular ones are no great fans of yours.'

'You could at least have told me.'

'I didn't tell you because I didn't want to be embarrassed about not inviting you. If you'd come along I know exactly what would've happened. You would've spent your time watching me, you would've tried to make me fall out with my friends or with my boyfriend, you would've done your best to ruin my holiday. I know you better than anyone, I've seen your jealousy, your paranoia, your weirdness. You really think I was going to put up with all that again? I'm afraid not.'

'But I'd no idea where you were. I was worried.'

'OK, Charlene. Let's stop this bullshit. You're going to listen to me for once. Get it into your thick skull that we aren't friends any more. We haven't been for a long time. But since you don't seem to be able to face up to this, I'm going to have to be blunt. You mean nothing to me. You've given me nothing. Maybe we had a bit of a laugh for a while, back when I was twelve or thirteen, but that's it. The rest counts for nothing. I don't give a shit about you, about your life, about what you think. I'll forget you very quickly, so you don't need to worry about me. If you can't forget me then that's too bad, but I really don't care.'

'Don't! Don't say that . . . After all I've done for you.'

'Please! Don't start that again. It doesn't work any more. You can't make me give in by threatening suicide or any crap like that.'

'. . .'

'So you've got nothing to say?'

'I'm sorry.'

'I knew you were going to say that. You've been saying you're sorry for years. For God's sake, have you had a look at yourself recently, Charlene? I've put up with your fucked-up-teenager psychodramas for four years now, and I've had enough, OK? I've grown up, you haven't. I've done everything I can for you but it hasn't helped. You just won't open up.'

'Sarah!'

'In six months I'm off to the States, they've given me a scholarship to go and study there. It's not everyone who gets that chance. I'm off for good.

My mother's coming with me, my boyfriend too, even my father wants to get back in touch with us. But don't kid yourself for one moment that you'll get me to change my mind and stay. I'm leaving to go and live a new life, to live for the people I love. I'm leaving to get away from you. Your presence has held me back. You're still a kid. I can't be responsible for you any more. It's got to the point where I can't even breathe without you standing behind me. You're suffocating me. I've got better things to be getting on with now than helping you. Charlene, we're just too different, you and me. I need space, I need life. You only know how to live as though you're in prison. I can't grow if you're always hanging onto me. You're suffocating me. Leave me alone. Goodbye.'

There was a dull thump and then nothing. No more voice, no more Sarah, nothing but a void and the intermittent sound of the electronic pulse that I listened to for several minutes before hanging up.

I didn't cry, I didn't scream, I didn't do anything. I just got changed, gave my hair a quick brush, pushed my sunglasses up onto my forehead and slung my bag over my shoulder.

'I'm going out, Mum. Don't wait up for me.'

I closed the door behind me and started walking, my steps resounding on the burning cobblestones. I went as far as the Café de l'Harmonie. The chimes tinkled as I pushed open the door. I looked around and saw Maxime. He was sitting at a table and staring out into the street.

'Can I sit down?'

He turned to face me. He'd never looked at me like that before. In the light of the sun coming in through the window, it seemed I was seeing his eyes for the first time. I'd never noticed just how blue they were, a deep midnight blue. An unspeakable pain was etched into them. I felt a lump constricting my throat.

I sat down without waiting for his answer. I lit the last cigarette in my packet and ordered a lemonade. I waited for him to speak, I wasn't able to say anything.

'Where were you? I called you at least a hundred times, I wrote you twenty letters in a single month. But not a word, nothing. I was worried stiff about you. I imagined the worst until I made myself admit that you'd maybe just forgotten me... That's it, isn't it? You've forgotten about me.'

'Maxime . . .'

I put my hand on his. The icy response shocked me. I kept on looking into his eyes but saying nothing, as though the silence might calm things. I stubbed out my butt in the ashtray and asked him if we could go somewhere else. He stood up and took me by the hand. We left the café and walked in silence to his apartment block, to his deserted apartment, to his room.

After we'd done it, I lay there and looked at him.

'So it's over?' he asked.

I nodded.

'It's better this way. It's best for both of us,' I said.

'You've made your decision. There's nothing more I can do,' he said quietly, without looking at me.

'I'm glad you understand.'

'What are you going to do now?'

'You don't need to worry about me.'

'I'm there for you, you know. You can always count on me.'

'You've already done enough for me, Maxine. Go and live your life. Forget me. That's the last thing I'll ask from you.'

I wiped the tears from his eyes and then stood up. I got dressed, set my sunglasses on my forehead, fixed my hair and picked up my bag. I left without looking back.

I'd done it.

Now that I'd left Maxime, now that I'd finally saved him from me, I was free and could concentrate on the one thing that was keeping me going.

Watching You Sleep

I needed to get my thoughts in order. I needed to withdraw from the world to be able to contemplate the situation calmly and draw up a plan of action. I needed to foresee all possible scenarios, to anticipate events in the greatest detail so as not to be caught off guard. Everything had to be perfect. If in my life I was to carry out just one act without messing up, this must be it.

I'd made the most important decision of my life. Of course, things would have been a lot simpler if I'd chosen to forget Sarah like she told me to, and had gone on loving Maxime. I would've lived the life he'd mapped out for us, a flat, banal sort of existence made up of love, children, work, and all the rest. Happiness, I suppose. But would I really have been saved? You can't escape your madness by making yourself act like a normal person. Your madness will always resurface. I gave in to mine. I saw that yielding was the only way to silence it. I cared nothing for the consequences, I wanted only to break free.

I knew exactly what I was doing. I knew it was terrible and unforgivable, that doing such a thing at the age of sixteen was unthinkable. I thought also of the sorrow and the humiliation it would inflict on my family and on Maxime, on the people who'd given me everything to try and help me be happy. I thought about the mess it would make of my own life, about the consequences, the trouble, the anguish, the shame, the weight of an act that would hang over me till the end of my days. But I knew I was helpless, that it was stronger than me and that I couldn't escape it. I knew that the few gestures required to complete this awful act were my only option. I had made my horrible decision and there was no turning back.

I learnt the whole routine off by heart, in my mind I practised every movement required. I rehearsed every day of the month that preceded that long-awaited September evening. I lived only in expectation of that ultimate moment.

The night of Thursday, 7 September finally arrived.

It was quite late but the café terraces were still full, the pedestrianised streets still filled with people, the city full of its usual sounds, as though Paris was refusing to rest for the night.

From my room I looked out at the street, the greyish roofs, the chimney stacks. The city was beautiful that evening. The sky, bathed in a fading light tinged with cinnamon and red, was unusually clear for September. Here and there a little cloud hovered over a rooftop. I felt as though someone up there was looking down at me, spying on me. Then something strange happened. For the first time in my life I began to pray. I sat on the window ledge, my eyes closed and soaked in silent tears, told God I was about to kill and asked for his forgiveness.

I waited for the sun to set, keeping watch at the window, waiting for the crowds to thin. I was scared. I felt that strange sensation you get, that knot that tightens in your stomach, just before the crucial moment, when your goal is within reach. A thin film of sweat covered my hands and my back. Once I left my bedroom, there would be no going back.

My parents had been asleep for at least the past three hours, they wouldn't hear anything. I climbed out of the window. The sound of my footsteps broke the silence of the streets. The night was mild. No other night I had seen in my life was like this night. It seemed to me that all the eyes in the world were on me, on my frail little silhouette that advanced over the cobblestones.

I arrived at Sarah's building. I knew that she always left her bedroom window open. The only difficulty would be in climbing up to her first-floor apartment. I looked around for her mother's Peugeot 106 but didn't see it. It was around two in the morning; I knew Martine never arrived home before dawn. I prayed that tonight would be no exception. I felt my heart thump against my chest so hard I thought it would burst through. I took a deep breath and closed my eyes for a moment. A last chance to take stock. I heard the little voice inside me: 'Go on. You're nearly there. What are you waiting for?'

I went for it. I stuck to my plan. I climbed over the street gate. Then along the garden path to the ground-floor terrace in front of the house, and, using the trellis and the Virginia creeper that grew on it, up to the balcony. So far so good. Then I slipped a little on the trellis and the noise woke the people who lived on the ground floor. I saw their light come on and froze, gripping the balcony rail with my damp hands. But after a minute or so the light was switched off. Carefully I swung myself up onto the balcony and stood at the window of Sarah's apartment.

It was open. I could hear her breathe as she slept, I could almost hear her dreams. Silently I drew aside the curtains and went into the room where I'd shared so many nights and so many secrets with her. As I moved slowly towards her I could almost hear the girlish whisperings from the time when we were friends.

She was stretched out on the mattress on the ground, her head on the bolster, her left hand over her face, her right on the cover. She didn't wake. I sat down in front of her to look at her in her rest.

I picked up a pillow. I wanted to close my eyes for a moment but I forced myself to keep them open. I had to be fully conscious of what I was doing.

Then I brought everything to a halt: time, the silence, the purity of sleep, the calm of night. I slammed the pillow down on her face with all my strength. She convulsed. Beneath me I felt her struggling body, her panicked arms and legs, her screams smothered by the pillow. I maintained the pressure. Her hands gripped my wrists but I was stronger than her. I pushed the pillow down harder. The whole thing lasted just a few minutes, yet the images of my action still fill my head. I had to be the victor for every single second. My body dominated hers. I was filled with a sensation of ecstasy, a momentary lack of consciousness, a feeling that I'd stepped outside of myself. The only thing that mattered was the pillow on her face and my hands on the pillow. Nothing else existed. I had created a vacuum. And I had won.

I reacted only much later, I'm not sure exactly how long after her hands let go of mine. Exhausted, suffocated, her body had finally yielded. When I saw that it was done, that my hands had stopped her breath, that her body was lifeless, only then did I realise that I had killed Sarah.

I removed the pillow and screamed in silence

when I saw her livid, lethargic face so close to me. I closed my eyes to block out the death I had caused. For a moment I thought I saw myself lying there asleep, next to the motionless body. Nausea took hold of me. I left Sarah lying stretched out on the sheets as though she were still sleeping and clambered out of the window. I walked out through the garden without looking back. When I got to the street I started running. I could see nothing but the dark of the night that was devouring me. I'd only gone about a hundred metres when I stopped to puke into a rubbish bin.

Four days later, around five in the afternoon, I was on my way home. It was a fine afternoon, the sort you hope for every day when school is over. I've just started my final year, I've picked the economics stream. I've been studying for the past two hours. I feel virtuous when I look at the pile of papers, photocopies, books, notes, the low-fat yoghurt and the copy of *Vingt Ans* magazine on my desk. I've left the window open and the new curtains I put up the day before billow in the gentle breeze.

It's nearly eight when the doorbell rings. My parents aren't at home tonight. This disturbance irritates me. I hurry to the hall door and open it to a tall, thin figure who stands there with his hands in his pockets and his eyes staring into space.

'Hi, Maxime.'

He moves closer to me. His face is serious,

impassive. I haven't seen him in two months. He's lost weight. God, he's changed so much since we last met. He's wearing trousers that are too big for him, a tailored shirt with a weird pattern on it, and a frock coat, all of which makes him look pretty original but doesn't suit him at all.

I rise up on to the tips of my toes, kiss him quickly on each cheek, and invite him in.

'Sit down . . .'

'No thanks. I'd prefer to stand.'

'OK.'

He looks down at the ground and says nothing. Maybe he's waiting for me to ask the reason for this unexpected visit. But instead I start talking about myself, about my teachers, my friends, about the café. He isn't listening.

'What about you?'

'Not much. I'm in the mathematics option but I don't like it. I might drop out. I'm fed up with school.'

Then he says he has a new girlfriend, she's called Marianne and she lives in the same building as him. He says it's going fine but he doesn't know if it'll last.

He stops and lifts his big eyes from the floor, looks at me for a few seconds, and then says in his faint, slow, slightly smoky voice: 'They found Sarah's body yesterday morning, in her room. Her mother found it. She'd been away for a few days. Suffocated.'

I was nonplussed. My life, my senses, my reason all came to a halt while around me everything spun wildly. I was lost, I was nowhere. I couldn't think. I didn't know how to react, I pretended I was stunned by the news. The truth was that I was screaming from pain because Maxime had been able to lay my soul bare, and I had not seen it coming.

'They know it was murder,' he said to break the silence. 'The police have begun an investigation. We'll see what they come up with.'

'I . . . I just don't know what to say . . .'

'I walked by her place last night. There were cops everywhere, so many people I couldn't really see anything.'

'Who could have done it? I mean, I . . . It's just so awful.'

'Stop it, Charlene.'

He didn't need to say any more. Nor did I.

Closing my eyes calms me a little. Maybe when I open them again everything will have disappeared. I can't bear to look at Maxime. I imagine him standing there next to me, imperturbable and tortured, his eyes accusing me and asking for forgiveness at the same time. I can feel him tremble, I sense him gathering all his strength so as not to show how shaken he is.

I've forgotten to breathe. I don't know what to do. The first sobs take a while arriving. Then they come thundering through my body, tearing at my throat and at my chest. I don't even know why I'm

crying. I don't know any more why I'm guilty, I don't know any more why I killed.

Maxime doesn't say anything, he moves closer to me. He looks at me, calms my fear, my anger and my shame by taking me in his arms and hugging me. He waits patiently till I've quietened down, till I get my breath back.

'What are you going to do now?' I manage to say.

'I've tried, Charlene. But I can't do anything more, I feel helpless, cowardly, weak. I'm obsessed by you. You can't even imagine how much I wish I didn't love you, how much I hate myself for being so powerless. I understand you but I can't help you. I won't do anything. I can't do anything any more. I've done all I can to help you love life. But you were too strong for me, or maybe it was Sarah who was too strong for me. I don't know. But I know you better than anyone else, Charlene. You hide from people, you run away all the time. I wanted to be able to share your world with you. But I can't. You needed me for a while, now you refuse my help. What I have to do now is to make myself forget you, chase you out of my life, accept your decision. And that's what I'll do. But what do you want me to do after that? You must decide that, and now. All I can say is that I'll never betray you, Charlene. Never. I'll pretend I know nothing. I'll stick to that story. I knew straight away what would happen. I knew even before you did. I knew you'd have to kill her to be able to feel free. But I'll stay silent. I'll remove myself from your life as quietly as I entered it.'

I couldn't look at him. My body was again seized by convulsions. I struggled to squeeze out my words.

'Tell me what I have to do.'

He took my wrists in his hands and stared at me, as though to tame my hatred and to make the truth come out of me.

'Charlene. Look me in the eyes and tell me you're sorry for what you did.'

My sobbing stopped in an instant. I kept my head down, I didn't want him to see my face. I couldn't tell him. How could I explain that I felt no remorse, that despite the pain, the hatred and the shame, I had emerged forever victorious from a life that I'd detested?

READING GROUP GUIDE

1. In the beginning of the novel, Charlene asks, "Would I have turned out a different person had my family circumstances been different?" How would you describe Charlene's relationship with her family? Was her childhood typical?

2. Charlene says that Vanessa is the only person who has always stayed close to her. Can you explain why Charlene feels so close to Vanessa, even though they only knew each other when they were both very young?

3. Why do you think Sarah visits Charlene in the hospital after the suicide attempt? Do you think that she really wanted to help Charlene?

4. Charlene and Sarah's relationship begins to deteriorate during the summer Sarah visits Vendee. That summer, Charlene writes Sarah everyday and Sarah writes one short postcard. How do these two different correspondence styles symbolize the two girls?

5. At the New Year's Eve party, Sarah cruelly locks Charlene in a closet. Why do you think Charlene continues to be friends with Sarah, even after this event?

6. In the bookstore when she meets Maxime, Charlene buys *A Psychological Study of Obsessional Murder*. Do you think Charlene knew then that she would kill Sarah? Or, do you think this book influenced Charlene's actions?

7. Maxime is a kind, loving, and understanding young man. Do you think that Charlene loves Maxime? How does he represent "what could have been" in Charlene's life?

8. At the end of the novel, Charlene leaves hundreds of messages on Sarah's answering machine and writes many letters. Do you consider Charlene's behavior stalking? If you were in Sarah's position, would you have gone to the police?

9. After murdering Sarah, Charlene claims that she has no remorse. Do you believe her?

10. Why do you think this novel is titled *Breathe*?

For more reading group suggestions visit
www.stmartins.com